I0680579

The Mountain and The Hammer

Meeks Kolich

Pandamonium Publishing House

Published in Canada by Pandamonium Publishing House™
www.pandamoniumpublishing.com
pandapublishing8@gmail.com

DEDICATION

For the people who suffer in silence.

For Hellen Keller.

For the people who teach the silent.

Above all for Anne Sullivan.

CONTENTS

Act I: BREAKFAST

BREAKFAST BEGINNING

On long journeys under the sun, one must bring life.
One must bring water. - A

At the strike of seven a.m., in an alleyway on the side of an old apartment building, a homeless man relieved his bladder. The leech of a man found significant joy in the fact that his stream was striking a flower.

Five floors above the deflowered dandelion, lay a girl. Sheltered in her warm room, Sophia Reeves slept peacefully. The warm apartment room contained a comfortable twin bed, a quaint nightstand, two potted plants and an old but sturdy desk. From atop the desk the low humming of a mechanical fan could be heard. A couple pieces of Sophia's professional photography equipment were also strewn about on the desk. The room also featured a decent sized closet, a dull ceiling light and a window facing the main road. Through the window, the dazzling morning sun was just beginning to appear.

"RRRrrrrrr!" began suddenly.
Sophia's hazel eyes opened with vigilance. She searched for the origin of the noise. As her eyes reached the ceiling the obtrusive sound stopped for
a moment.

"The fucking thing died again!" yelled a voice right above Sophia. The voice was muffled but loud enough to be understood.

Ugh what time is it? thought Sophia Reeves. *Why do the Mulligans have to vacuum right now?*

She grabbed her cell phone off the nightstand and saw it was 7:07 a.m.

Angrily, she rolled her eyes and then placed the cell phone on the pillow beside her head. Sophia laid back down, kept her eyes open and prepared for what was to come.

"RRRrrrrr! RRRrrrrrrrr! RRRrrrrrrrrrrrrrrrrr..." Went the vacuum right above Sophia's head. "Ha! Hey! HEY! I GOT IT TO WORK AGAIN!" Bellowed Mr. Mulligan.

Although it could not be heard anymore, the low hum of the mechanical fan continued at its unceasing pace. Ten minutes later Sophia was reawakened. She awoke surprised. Her ears could still hear Mr. Mulligan's vacuum. It was now accompanied by his stomping feet. Before a conscious thought entered her head, Sophia's stomach grumbled loudly. At the same time, the mechanical fan turned off.

Presently, Sophia sat up in her bed. Her arms reached high above her head. This was a ritual gesture she performed when she awoke from a pleasant rest. While reaching high above her head she imagined that she was unplugging the annoying vacuum. *I'd tie his shoelaces together if I could*, Sophia thought menacingly. While smiling deviously she realized she was nude. Her nakedness did not surprise her. However, she had the distinct memory of falling asleep with one of her bras on. Regardless Sophia's chest welcomed the lack of restriction during this blissful stretch. Finishing up, Sophia observed her desk. She saw that her pink lace bra was atop the simple deactivated mechanical fan. Additionally, her notebook and photography equipment lay in utter disarray.

Above Sophia, Mr. Mulligan moved his vacuuming into a different room. Although it could still be heard, it had become much more tolerable. Sophia wiped the sleep from her eyes. She glanced to her cell phone. As if activated by her sight the device vibrated.

"Hmmm...I wonder how much I made from last night," purred Sophia in a temperate voice.

By turning on her cell Sophia catalogued this Sunday morning's notifications. She had received: four Paypal emails confirming twenty-one-dollar payment, ten Instagram notifications, nine Twitter notifications, eight FairySnap notifications, and a single text message. From her mother.

Sophia unlocked her phone and opened her mother's text message. It read: "Good morning my beloved daughter, I hope you had a good sleep! I'm driving the 51 route this morning, but I'll be home for dinner. Eat something for breakfast. Love you."

Sophia could not muster the will to respond to her mother right away. Nor clean up her desk. Nor get something to eat. The desire to fall back asleep nagged at her. Instead, she hit her phone's home button. Then she tapped the apple music app, searched for J. Cole and selected *No Role Modelz*.

...

On the same Sunday, at 6:57a.m. a short stout woman sat in the driver seat of bus 018. Marge Reeves wore her ordinary blue spring uniform with her matching blue HSR baseball cap with black sunglasses. She took a generous swallow of her morning coffee from the poppy red travel mug her daughter bought her.

"Large Marge!" said a jovial voice.

With her attention pulled away from her coffee, Marge turned and looked out the open bus doors.

"Zeke," said Marge with a controlled smile. "We're waiting for you."

A tall, unkept man sauntered onto the bus. Zeke stank of stale beer. His black hair was disheveled and there were wet stains drying out on his clothes. An ancient jean jacket and equally old jeans. In his hands were two black garbage bags filled with crushed beer cans. And on his back was a black Jansport backpack.

As Zeke paid the bus fare Marge said, "Those university kids sure love to drink, eh?"

"And don't you go telling anyone else, Large Marge," said Zeke with wink. "These bags is gonna become a new bike. A brand-new baby blue bike!"

"I like your energy this morning Zeke. Well, the faster you sit down the faster you can be sitting on your new bike," replied Marge.

The malodorous gentleman nodded and chose a seat close to the back exit of the bus and at 7:01 a.m. bus 018, 51 University, began its Sunday morning route.

BAD
BREAKFAST

In times of great stress, we become what we know we are. - A

On the same day, the Cavallone family was in the middle of a serious family talk. A sober dialog that would change the Cavallone family dynamic forever.

An hour before the talk, Carmine Cavallone sat alone in his restaurant kitchen. He was accompanied by a fresh bag of tomatoes and a chef's knife. As he adjusted his glasses, he began to hum a melancholy tune. The familiar chop of his knife was uninterrupted as the slices of tomatoes fell.

The humble kitchen was supplied with the basic necessities to run a family restaurant. Carmine inherited the family business from his parents and decided to keep the kitchen floor plan the same as it always was. Tradition kept the space organized in an efficient manner that prioritized function. However, Carmine had been slowly modernizing the infrastructure. He conducted his work at the new robust kitchen table. Additionally, a faint buzz of electricity was identifiable from the freshly installed industrial fridge and a state-of-the-art commercial stove.

...

Thirty minutes before the talk, Arianna Cavallone finished tidying the dining area of the restaurant. She observed the space. She thought that the dining area screamed 'Italian family restaurant.' While the thought was over exaggerating, the aesthetic was firmly established.

At the back of the dining area, beside the beige kitchen doors, was a quaint modest bar. It was supplied with a battalion of authentic Italian wines. A few were quite rare. At its corner sat a faux 2006 Italian FIFA world cup champions trophy. Behind it, on the wall, was a proud Italian flag.

Like the kitchen, the dining area also prioritized function and therefore was expertly spaced. It had room for patrons and ample space for servers.

The tables and chairs were simple and practical. The tables were covered with a checkered patterned tablecloth, in russet and evergreen, and paired with comfortable wooden chairs. In the center of every table sat a small vase with hand-picked dandelions. A task that Arianna's youngest son completed.

Arianna's eyes lingered upon the dandelions as she reminisced. She recalled the time she found her son ripping dandelions from the earth.

...

"Lo'! What are you doing? Why are you doing that?" Arianna asked.

"It's for school," replied Lorenzo Cavallone, in a matter-of-fact tone.

"Is it now?"

"An art project."

"Well then, steady as she goes." And after a moment of pause, "But we should catch up with your father and brother. The trail has turned, and I can't see them anymore."

"I confidently agree. Family hikes through the fall forest should be done together."

"You know what?"

"What?"

"I just had an idea. Pick out enough dandelions for each table, back home. Would you do that for me?"

"Mooooom! There's like seventy million tables at home. Woah! Okay! Okay, I'll do it. Holy! Just don't give me your death stare."

...

Lo's hands were caked with mud, Arianna thought. She shook her head softly and then walked past the tables and chairs to the main entrance. To the left of the main entrance Arianna opened the thick curtains with the pull of a string. The dining area was dispelled of darkness by the sun's dazzling rays.

Arianna's attention was pulled toward the melancholy humming that could be heard from the kitchen doors. She silently paced towards the sad sound and peered through the window on the door.

Through the glass, Arianna observed her husband sitting alone in the kitchen. His back was towards her. Arianna thought his spine stood straight as an arrow. As she stood outside the kitchen doors his humming filled her with the feeling of sorrow.

...

Twenty minutes before the talk, directly above the kitchen, there was a firm knock on a pitch-black wooden door.

"Breakfast in ten," said a confident voice. "I'm finished with the washroom. All yours."

On the other side of the pitch-black door was a young boy. Lorenzo Cavallone was awake and under the covers of his bed. He was scrolling through Instagram on his phone when he heard his older brother call out to him from beyond his door. He heard his brothers' solid footsteps recede.

Lorenzo hit his phone's home button and focused on the time. It read 9:03 a.m. He produced a weak sigh and then placed his phone down on the bed.

While still under the covers he stretched his neck. When his left ear almost touched his left shoulder, his neck released a crack. This caused a fox-like smile to appear on his face. As Lorenzo's right ear came closer to his right shoulder no sound was produced.

Violently, Lorenzo removed his covers. He threw his blanket off him as if the touch of the cloth offended him. It landed in a jumble at the foot of his bed. He enjoyed beginning his day in an unagreeable mood.

Lorenzo hung legs over the edge of the bed and began searching the floor wildly. He donned his slippers and braced his eyes. His left hand reached out to the wall and pressed a switch. With the speed of light Lorenzo's room was illuminated. The florescent lightbulb above him glowed.

"Ugh," said Lorenzo's sleepy voice.

There he sat for a brief moment. Lorenzo had fallen asleep wearing a pair of soccer shorts and his favourite band t-shirt. The black cloth hung loosely on his body. He enjoyed wearing larger fitted clothing. The large black shirt displayed the image of a fearsome hydra and, across the chest, the name *Snake Detection Hypothesis.* One of the hydra heads was wearing sunglasses and another had a scar over its left eye.

Lorenzo got up, left his phone on his bed, and opened his door. Straight ahead of Lorenzo was the empty washroom. He noticed that someone had left the window open. The bright sunlight made the room appear fresh. This effected Lorenzo's downcast mood.

Down the hall, he saw his older brother exit his room. Lorenzo noticed his brother's calm demeanour. He also observed that Liam Cavallone was wearing his black collar work shirt with the button's undone, revealing a crisp white undershirt. Liam paired this with black work shorts that revealed his muscular legs. On his feet were slippers that matched his own.

"Morning bro," said Lorenzo.

"Good morning, Lo," replied Liam with a smile. "I'm going to help dad with breakfast. You should come down a.s.a.p."

Liam accentuated every letter by poking Lorenzo playfully on the forehead. At the last letter Lorenzo caught his brother's finger. They both smiled and Lorenzo let it go.

"Yes Captain," said Lorenzo.

Liam ruffled his little brother's hair and, in a sarcastic tone, said, "Oh Captain, my captain." Liam then passed by his brother and walked downstairs.

As Lorenzo used the washroom and got prepared for the day, he recalled last Sunday's movie night. The Cavallone family had watched *Dead Poet's Society*. Chiefly for two main reasons. It was Liam's theatre and film homework and to honor the unforgettable Robbin Williams. Last Sunday, in the living room, the family surrounded the bleeding-edge flat screen T.V.

...

"*Patch Adams, Mrs. Doubtfire, G-*" listed off Carmine confidently.

"Don't you dare forget *Good Will Hunting*," quickly interrupted Arianna.

"I was literally going to say that next," returned Carmine, "It was on the tip of my to-"

"He was also a genie," commented Lorenzo in-between bites of popcorn.

"Oi! Can we actually watch the movie?" Cut in Liam defiantly. "This is going to be a quiz tomorrow!"

"Liam, look, we can rewind it sweetie," offered Arianna diplomatically.

"Simmer down, son," said Carmine. "They were just walking around. Lo' when did he play a genie?"

"Ummm," thoughtfully sounded Lorenzo. "Aladdin! He was the voice of the genie."

"Oh yeah! I love Disney movies. How could I have forgotten that?" said Carmine.

"When did he pass away again? It was such a tragedy," asked Arianna.

"MA! Holy moly! I swear I'm gonna pass away, can we pleeease watch the movie?"

"Alright, alright hold your horses! We get it," said Arianna. "No more chatter from the peanut gallery."

"Is silence during a movie too much to for ask for?" questioned Liam rhetorically.

...

Meanwhile, downstairs, in the kitchen, Carmine, Arianna, and Liam were seated at the robust kitchen table. Carmine's prep work for the restaurant was finished and stashed away. And thanks to Arianna's organization, the dining room was prepared to receive customers.

Before them on the table was a breakfast of scrambled eggs, sausages, buttered toast, and orange juice. However, none of them were eating. In fact, the direction of the conversation squashed their appetite.

...

Lorenzo nonchalantly made his way down the stairs. He crossed the bar and opened the kitchen doors.

"So, to sum it all up, you're both thinking 'bout getting a divorce," offered Liam.

Lorenzo swallowed in his dry throat. He noticed his brother sitting with his back to him and his parents on either side of the table. Lorenzo's intense gaze searched his mother's face and saw her rueful expression. Liam's eyes followed his father's left hand. It grasped his forehead and wiped down to his chin. His glasses sat on the table in front of him.

Utterly flabbergasted, Lorenzo asked, "You're getting divorced?"

BREAKFAST
BOUNTIFUL

If your family commands it, is it not so? - A

A plethora of birds chirped playfully. Dull brown, bright blue and sharp red feathers splashed lively from the elegant garden fountain in the Singh's backyard. Behind the fountain two young squirrels chased one another around the old maple tree, and along the perimeter, several bumble bees buzzed softly as they floated from flower to flower.

The Singh family backyard was well maintained. The garden itself was meticulously tended to. It was the pride and joy of Kunal Singh. Jiya Singh, Kunal's wife, liked to joke and call it The Garden of Eden. Mind you, in an extremely solemn way. In such a manner that did, in fact, make the joke hilarious. Kunal would politely laugh at the constant comment. To date, he counts eighty-eight times that joke has been said. However, all jokes contain a varying degree of truth. And on a Sunday like today, with the sun shining brightly, the garden looked heavenly.

Kunal and Jiya had been married for twenty-seven years. They met in India while attending university. Some years later, a bachelor's degree, a master's degree, a blessed stroke of luck, and some light networking had developed into tenures at McMaster University.

During the time of university employment, order was established. However, a time of chaos followed. It came in the form of marriage and childbirth. Their son was speaking presently.

"Yes mother," said a voice that was still getting used to its new deepness. "I made sure to apply for all three programs at McMaster last night. I completed the task with a classmate."

Raza Singh, an only child, sat with proper posture on an exquisite metal mesh patio chair. A table that was furnished with a

Singh traditional breakfast; buttered and spiced potatoes, fresh flatbread, hummus and lightly salted scrambled eggs.

Jiya finished sipping at her orange juice and said, "I hope the friend aiding you in this endeavor was not Liam Cavallone. Everyone knows he's a fantastic soccer player but he's not the sharpest tool in the shed." Her voice was characteristically timid. Yet her words were anything but.

"Liam's intelligence shines when he leads," replied Raza. "Out on the pitch it's as clear as the weather we get to enjoy today."

"Everyone has their own unique strengths...and unique weaknesses," added Kunal. His husky voice emanated from behind the Sunday paper he had been scanning.

"My point exactly, honey," said Jiya. She nodded once and readjusted her posh sunglasses.

Raza swallowed a mouthful of flatbread and hummus. He asked, "Can I get back to presenting my evidence? In defense that I actually applied to post-secondary education."

He understood his parents' silence as confirmation to proceed with his case.

"The classmate I applied with was Sophia. Sophia Reyes. In fact, I agreed to tutor her in biology as well."

"Hmm. Raza, my dear, you're putting a lot on your plate," commented Jiya passively.

"I'm almost finished my plate," hastily riposted Raza.

"Your mother is speaking about your plate of commitments. Not the plate in front of you," said Kunal. "You air head."

With obvious discontent Raza said, "Ah, I see."

Suddenly, Kunal Singh lowered the Sunday paper. It made a tremendous ruffling noise that sent a gust of wind across the table. He revealed a thick black beard, a full toothed grin and smiling eyes. Raza witnessed this and his sorrow was immediately replaced with a copy of his father's delight. Professor Kunal Singh was known to tease without malice.

"I jest," Kunal said jovially. "Here. Check out these jughead comics. They're a hoot."

He folded the paper in half and handed it across the table to his son.

Kunal continued, "And with regards to Raza's schedule, he is doing fine. Pah! Your mother, my sweet young flower here... Hey! I can see your eyes roll off the table." He pointed a finger at his son. "Raza, pick up your eyes and observe that her criticism derives from love."

"Yes. Love of course," said Raza half-heartedly. "Honestly, I'd prefer more lecturing and less flirting from the professors. Please...I will beg."

"Oh, grow up!" returned Jiya. "The sight of true love transforms you intoa witty imp."

Jiya removed her sunglasses emphatically. She revealed her grey eyes and an ice-cold expression.

"Should we apologize for our love? Hmm? That your two old, decrepit, decaying parents are still capable of displaying the fundamental human emotion known as love. We are still human beings. We also happen to be your parents. Hmph! Our displays of love are innate! Instinctive even! They are essential to what it means to be alive."

At the end of her emotional outburst, without making eye contact, Kunal and Jiya joined hands.

"Your mother asks rhetorical questions," said Kunal. He then turned his attention to his wife. His eyes looked lovingly into hers.

The sight of this repulsed Raza profoundly and he made a conscious decision not to hide it.

"She does indeed," replied Raza. "Because the intended answer is yes. You truly should apologize for it."

...

Outside the canopy there were no clouds in the sky. The colourful birds were now up high drying off in the bright sun. The two squirrels were now searching for food and the old maple tree enjoyed the peaceful state of the Singh backyard.

Raza Flashback

Kindly imagine a massive flash. A flash that consumed your entire vision. Had you anticipated it, you would have chosen to close your eyes. Unfortunately, you did not. And once your vision returned, it returned without the ability to distinguish color.

I find it pleasing to be here. While this is a pseudo form of my realm it is equally reinvigorating. A breath of fresh air if you will.

Did you enjoy meeting the main actors? It's my earnest desire that you did.

Where are we exactly?

Allow me to promptly explain the situation.

We will be going on a field trip of sorts. All that is required of you is to play the obedient passenger. I will dutifully drive us through this space. And remember it's a place that lacks color. That does not mean it lacks distinction.

I find that truly intriguing. The realm of memory is painted with shades of grey. Memories, which cause such colorful emotions, exist in a space without any. Enough woolgathering! Let us begin the flashback.

...

Raza Singh's single most cherished memory took place at a tournament. Specifically, a male youth soccer tournament. Further preciseness: during a game that would result in zero consequences.

Fate had produced a fissure in this year's tournaments schedule. One team was disqualified for truly unruly behaviour. And so, with much shuffling and rearranging, a round of soccer games was played that would in no way affect the end results of the tournament.

The staff of the event informed the coaches and Raza's coach, Roy Mustang, decided to tell his team right before the fateful match.

"Good afternoon gentlemen," began coach Mustang. His voice came out cool and composed. "I require your keen attention. That means no more talk about the Titans. What they did was shameless and disgraceful. Davys and Mathews! That's enough. Pay attention," Mustang said coldly. "I have significant news regarding this match."

Coach Mustang spoke to them while they were all seated on the bench just outside the field of play. That year, Raza's soccer team was the Eagles.

Mustang continued dutifully, "Due to the actions of those who were ejected from the tournament, this game is worth no points."

He allowed a moment for his team to comprehend this.

"Yes. Win or lose. The result will not affect where we finish in this tournament. Over there, the other coach is telling his team this right now."

Comically, at the same time, the entire Eagles team bench looked over at the other team.

"That said, this game provides us a unique opportunity. The opportunity to be creative. We still have the rest of the tournament ahead of us. However, this game will be used as an experiment. If anyone would like to try out a different position, that will be arranged. Davy, if you happen to think Mathews is absolute trash at right wing, this game, you can show him how it's done." Mustang waited for their laughter to subside. "Defensemen! If you would like

*to play midfield or striker, the option is available. This game will not be remembered by the tournament. So how will **you** remember it?"*

...

Raza remembered this game with precise vividness. And for good reason. The game started like two New York alley cats meeting for the first time. Backs arched and tails puffed. However, things changed rapidly when Michael Santana scored on the Eagles. A perfectly timed header gave the Spartans the first goal of the game.

*Now, to be crystal clear, it was not the first goal that changed the atmosphere of the game. It was the **celebration** of the first goal that generated a dynamic shift in mood.*

Santana chose to celebrate his goal with genuine vigor, for two main reasons; first, this game did not matter, and second, he scored a truly stunning goal. So, after scoring, Michael Santana ran to the left corner flag and proceeded to complete the orange justice dance. I will add, he did so with supreme accuracy. These gyrations and frantic movements got the ball moving. Eight minutes later, it got the ball moving right into the Spartan's net.

The Eagles first celebration, fueled by revenge, was performed as if rehearsed. Mathews, the goal scorer, ran back to the center of the field and suddenly, with much exaggeration, flopped on the grass as a fish would. Not missing a beat, the defenseman ran over to him and mimed that they were reeling him in with a fishing rod. As soon as Mathews flopped over to them, they picked him up and presented him to Raza. Who in turn accurately mimicked taking a flash photo from a camera.

The effect of this performance was profound. It emboldens the Eagles. It enraged the Spartans. And lastly, it captivated the spectators. In fact, a parent of one of the Spartans commented, "What the fuck am I watching?"

Desiring a taste of glory, Raza asked one of the strikers if he could swap positions. Davy, affected by the atmosphere of the game, agreed to cover Raza's center midfield spot. Thus, the game continued with Raza playing forward, among other spur of the moment changes.

Back and forth they fought. The perceptive Eagles versus mighty Spartans. And with seven minutes left in play, Raza, the Eagle's ace, scored the final goal.

A perfect cutback pass found Raza in an undefended patch of grass. He was directly in front of the Spartan net. One breath later, Raza locked eyes with the Spartan's goalkeeper. Suddenly, the ball was struck. The ball moved with solid pace past the keeper into the back of the Spartan's net.

The referee's piercing whistle announced the authenticity of Raza's goal. It also began his celebration.

Quick long strides brought Raza to the corner flag. He crossed the boundary of play and settled down on his right knee. Directly in front of him was a girl. She was seated on a worn pink blanket with two other girls.

Raza's meticulous memory remembers the initial reaction of amused bewilderment on his target's face. Her eyes matched his gaze and then followed the movement of his hand. Raza mimed pulling out a small box. In an exaggerated fashion, he pretended to open it.

In response the girls' hands reached up and covered her mouth. It was just Raza's luck that he kneeled in front of the girl with a dream to become an actress. Silently, she then nodded her head three times. They stood together and embraced. The crowd clapped. Some with satire, others with genuine effort.

The fictitious newlyweds disengaged. Raza turned back to the field of play and saw the look of smugness on the referee's face. He then heard the whistle blown and saw a yellow card held high. According to the referee, Raza had violated the rule of leaving the field of play. However, he did not care one bit.

Act II: SATISFYING

STUDY
SESSION

One needs to learn how they learn to truly learn. - A

"It goes kingdom, phylum, class, order...hold up. Sophia, are you following along?" Raza asked.

Fifth period had just begun. Serendipitously, Sophia Reeves and Raza Singh had fifth period spare. The two youths had been studying biology for precisely five minutes when Raza questioned Sophia.

They were reviewing biology in their high school library, in one of the group study rooms. And like all the study rooms, the room was particularly drab. Dark grey carpet floors pared with eggshell white walls. Illuminated by four dim electric lights. The old, yet reliable, table was centered in the middle of the room and provided ample space for six individuals. Today it housed two.

On this day, Sophia's dark brown hair was in a high ponytail. The lobes of her ears were adorned with small black gemstones. She wore a fresh jean jacket over a pink flannel button down. Hidden by the sleeves of the jacket, a Pandora bracelet was fastened on her left wrist. Her white vans and favourite pair of jeans completed the ensemble.

Raza sat in a duplicate plastic high school chair directly opposite from Sophia. He had removed his plain black hoodie and wore a plain white long sleeve shirt. Adidas flip flops and black soccer shorts covered his lower half. Presently he scratched the back of his head and then ran his fingers through his short black hair.

"Ugh. Razaaa I'm obviously paying attention," replied Sophia. There was guilt in her voice and breast. Instead of reviewing her notes she had been online shopping. The tab of the purchase was still open. "You said we were reviewing the fundamentals of biology."

"Indeed. I did say that," confirmed Raza. A dash of annoyance entered his voice. "However, I said that minutes ago. We moved on to the system that classifies animals." His irritating feeling persisted. "You were the one who asked me for help. Why are we here if you aren't going to participate?"

Sophia ignored the desire to check her phone and said, "Okay you caught me." She sighed. "I'll come clean. I was online shopping. Here, take a look."

Sophia turned her laptop around in order for Raza to see. Raza's eyes focused on the screen. At the focal point of her laptop was an exquisite blue lingerie garment. Before he thought to look away, he saw a sensual velvet bra and panties. They were matched with a velvet robe and belt. He was reminded of waves on the beach, softly kissing the shore before it returned back to sea. His face became warm. Raza's eyes darted up to the left corner of the room before he could see the ludicrous price or website address.

"So, Raza, what do you think?" Asked Sophia in a perfectly innocent voice.

Currently, Raza's thoughts were jumbled and confused. He could not fathom Sophia wearing that kind of clothing. However, his mind provided him with possible positions and styles in which she could wear the presented attire. Raza swallowed and said, "I think you're distracting us from the goal of this study session."

Pouting, Sophia pressed on, "Does it not suit me?"

She was genuinely hurt. The garment spoke to her. She craved it and wanted a second opinion that agreed with her initial instinct. Raza was known as an athlete and an intellectual boy. His agreement would immediately push her to confirm payment.

Raza heard the pleading tone in her voice. He was not accustomed to this level of supplication. Subconsciously, as if he was on the field playing soccer, he quickly changed direction. "Did you hear about Kassandra McPherson?"

Raza was relieved to see Sophia's head tilt to the right. Taking the bait, she asked, "What happened to Kassandra McPherson?"

Sophia then turned her laptop back around and toyed with her bracelet.

"She was expelled yesterday," answered Raza. "Bruce Bigby told me in first period."

Sophia accepted this right away. Bruce played on the high school soccer team with Raza. Furthermore, Bruce's father was one of the vice principals.

The seriousness of the punishment sobered Sophia's flirtatious mood. "What did she do?" whispered Sophia.

"According to Mr. Bigby, she was caught with a FairySnap account," said Raza. He saw the keen look on Sophia's face. Raza then pulled out his phone, unlocked it, and showed Sophia the photo Bruce had sent him. "I'm not sure how he managed to get it, but Bruce sent me this as proof."

Sophia's eyes examined Raza's cell phone screen. Kassandra was laying on her bed in a provocative position. Her radiant blond hair cascaded from her head and exquisite make-up was painted on her face. The photo was edited in a manner that turned her mattress into a comforting bed of clouds. Additionally, fairy wings, made of light, were edited into the photo. They protruded from behind her. It was clear to Sophia that underneath Kassandra's silk white robe she was nude. With a click of a button the screen went black. Raza turned off his phone. He deemed Sophia had seen enough.

Sophia wet her lips with her tongue. "And she was expelled for this?" she asked.

"For the time being," Raza answered. He placed his phone face down on the table beside his laptop. He then crossed his arms against his chest and continued, "Bruce said his dad is conducting a thorough investigation. It's like, super serious. She's expelled for the time being but her father, Richard McPherson, is fighting the punishment profusely. He's saying her daughter was cosplaying. And that's her personal hobby. It's quite the interesting story."

Upon hearing this Sophia took an undignified swig from her

water bottle, "Wow," commented Sophia. This bemused Raza.

"Indeed, much wow," stated Raza. "Now may we get back to biology?"

SWEAT Y
STRETCH

A body knows before the mind does. - A

With both hands, Raza Singh shielded his eyes from the sun's luminous shine. The heat felt relentless today. A heat that came just before the changing of seasons. Promptly, Raza could feel a gust of wind blow through his hair and he was grateful for it. It was a calm cool breeze in the stifling weather.

"Hold for one...two...three," bellowed a confident voice.

With eyes still shielded, Raza looked to the owner of the voice. Ten feet away, Liam Cavallone stood tall with his hands raised together high above his head.

Liam stood at the center of a circle. It was composed of the senior boy's high school soccer team, which consisted of twenty-one students. Already, sweat was visible on most of the players. They had just finished doing laps around the soccer field and were stretching out. As usual, Liam, the official team captain, lead the boys through the stretching routine.

The cool breeze passed through the rest of the team. Raza witnessed grateful faces on most of his fellow teammates. Physically, Raza followed along. Mentally, he was following the wind. Raza watched keenly as he attempted to keep his eyesight on the movement of the swift zephyr. He could perceive its immediate movement through the green grass. The quick breeze was headed to the high school's second field. Over there the senior girl's rugby team were holding their tryouts. *Was it a practice or a tryout? I should have paid more attention to the announcements. And was it senior girls or junior girls? I can't see that far,* Raza thought to himself. While stretching, he recalled today's closing announcements.

...

Exactly thirty minutes ago, back in the monotonous library study room, Raza and Sophia were interrupted by the school bell. It rang in three short bursts to mark the end of the school day.

"The closing announcements are so bor-" said Sophia.

"Good day to you all," began Mr. Bigby. On the traditional P.A. system, his voice was loud and staticky. "These are the closing announcements. The senior girls' rugby tryouts begin today. The tryout will be held on the second field behind the senior boys' soccer practice. It's a hot one, so stay hydrated."

Sophia pointed at Raza and mouthed the words, "That's you." In response, Raza characteristically rolled his eyes.

While studying for the next biology chapter quiz, specifically chapter two: animals, Sophia had removed her jean jacket. Her dark brown high ponytail remained. Meanwhile, Raza had rolled up his white long sleeves to his elbows.

"Next announcement is directed towards the dress code!" Thundered Mr. Bigby's voice. "The recent trend of students dressed in revealing clothes stops now. We allow plenty of freedom and the weather *is* hot. However, this school demands *modest* attire. Not complying to this *standard* will result in dire consequences."

During this time Raza was acutely aware of Sophia's outfit. Her pink flannel shirt was fully unbuttoned. It exposed a tight white tank top. At the upper centre of the top was a blue bedazzled butterfly. Similarly, Sophia's eyes lingered on Raza's rolled up white sleeves.

"This is the **last verbal warning** you will be receiving."

Sophia's sensitive ear could hear Mr. Bigby emphasize his words. She suppressed a smile.

"If outfits do not meet dress code, you will be removed off the property. Full Stop. An immediate wave of suspensions and, in the most recent case, expulsion, has commenced."

In response to Mr. Bigby's pressing news, Sophia made sure

she had Raza's attention before she rolled her eyes in imitation of him. Raza blushed softly. To distract himself he quietly and quickly packed his belongings.

"And Today's Closing Announcement," said Mr. Bigby's voice. He paused for a brief moment, then said, "The way you handle yourself on social media directly reflects upon our school's name. Expulsions and Suspensions are our ways of displaying how serious we are about enforcing a modest dress code. Simply put, if you are not dressed for school, then you are going home." The P.A system was curtly turned off.

Sophia watched Raza finish packing his bag. "Thanks again for helping me study," she said sweetly. "I appreciate it. Hope soccer practice is fun," she said.

"Thanks," returned Raza. "It always is."

...

Back on the soccer field, under the mighty sun, Raza scratched the back of his head.

"Oi! Earth to Raza. Care to help me?" asked Liam Cavallone.

Without a word, Raza walked into the center of the circle. The soft grass was pierced by the spikes on his simple black cleats. When he approached Liam, they both raised their hands to their chests.

"Rock. Paper. Scissors!" They said in unison.

Raza went with paper. Liam chose scissors.

Liam smiled victoriously and Raza said, "Fine. Lay down."

The other boys surrounding Liam and Raza paired up and played the same game. The winners got to lay on the ground and get stretched out first.

Liam lay with his back on the grass. He raised his right leg to

Raza's chest. Raza caught Liam's leg with his hands. "Not too far," requested Liam.

Raza nodded his head once. "Cavallone commands," he said sarcastically.

Before Liam could respond Raza began stretching out his captain. Raza carefully pushed Liam's extended right leg towards his head.

"One...two...three...four," began Raza in a loud voice.

The other soccer players joined his counting on the even numbers.
However, Raza could hear giggling coming from a pair of boys at his back. At the count of ten they swapped legs and began the process with the other leg.

Raza began counting again, "One...two...three..."

At the count of ten Liam lowered his left leg and raised his right hand towards Raza. Raza took his hand and helped Liam to his feet.

As he stood tall Liam said, "Your turn."

Raza assumed the position Liam was previously in. The warm grass felt pleasant on Raza's back. Another fresh gust of wind blew through the stretching circle. Raza raised his left leg towards Liam's prepared hands.

Without warning a boy asked, "So is it true?"

While lying on the grass Bruce Bigby erupted with laughter.

"What's this about?" asked Liam. His voice was full of cold authority.

"Jamie is inquiring about Kassandra McPherson," answered Raza mildly.

Bruce, finished with his outburst, quickly added, "Yes, it's true. In fact, from one of the photos I saw of her, we could be cosplaying right now."

This comment brought a genuine smile to Raza's face. It also brought a scowl to Liam's face and hoots of laughter from some of the fellow soccer players.

One of the boys took this opportunity to bend over on all fours. When his rear was excessively pointed upwards, he exclaimed: "Look at me cosplay!"

Further laughter erupted from the soccer team. Bruce wiped tears from his eyes. Even Liam allowed himself a smile.

"If we have time for laughter, we have time for more laps!" Roared a mature voice.

The voice was a bolt of lightning. The levity of the senior boys' high school soccer team immediately vanished.

Coach Armstrong had silently paced towards his team and found them entranced by a spell of laughter.

This mountain of a man stood with his muscular arms crossed over his brawny chest. As usual, coach Armstrong wore his teaching attire. Today that meant a dress shirt with a maroon vest paired with slacks. Even while coaching, he rarely changed this outfit. His eyes were covered by reflective sunglasses.

"You've earned yourselves seven more laps around both fields," commanded coach Armstrong. "Was it a funny experience to lose our exhibition match?"

One player was attacked with a fit of coughing. When he was finished, Raza and Liam solemnly began leading their team in their enforced cardio punishment.

"And don't distract those female rugby players with your cosplay!" Armstrong yelled.

...

When the high school bell had rung three times, to mark the closing of the day, Lorenzo Cavallone was nowhere near to hear it. He was on the city bus, on his way to his friends' house. Lorenzo had decided to skip his fifth period class in order to get there earlier.

He had made this trip countless times and was prepared to distract himself. Through headphones, Lorenzo's ears were connected to his phone. "If It Means A Lot to You" by A Day to Remember played in his ears. While he listened to music, he doodled in his notebook.

"Pink + White" by Frank Ocean's began to play and Lorenzo lifted his head to observe his current surroundings; the bus was stopped at a red light, overhead, the sun shone magnificently. Through the bus window Lorenzo saw a group of high school kids on the sidewalk. They wore blue uniforms from a different school. Possibly catholic. One kid at the back of the group bounced a basketball. He noticed that some kids on the bus wore the same uniform.

Lorenzo returned his attention to his notebook. He continued with his drawing. His pencil accurately drew the hydra from his T-shirt. Each individual head was drawn with an expression of ferocity. One was even drooling venom. He was proud of his drawing. *Wicked*, thought Lorenzo.

The request to stop was sounded and it pulled Lorenzo's attention away from his notebook. He identified that his stop was after this one and so he got ready to depart.

"Sober" by Childish Gambino was cut off as Lorenzo wrapped up his headphones and mp3 player. Once it was safely put away, he pulled the cord to request the next stop. While the bus was still in motion he rose from his seat and moved to the rear exit. The bus stopped and the back door opened. Outside the door was a bus stop in front of a church.

"Thanks!" said Lorenzo to the bus driver. In response the bus driver silently waved his hand.

...

Eight minutes later, Lorenzo stood at the front door of a lavish house. The house belonged to the Zhang family. He took out his phone and texted four letters.

Seconds later, Lorenzo heard the garage door open. A brief moment later the massive white door had opened. He witnessed that the place had not changed since his last visit. Hanging from the roof was a disco ball. It was currently turned on. The comfortably furnished space was filled with smoke, darkness, and dancing lights.

This is where the Snake Detection Hypothesis practiced for gigs and hung out. The back of the garage was for band practice. It had a beautiful drum kit and, beside it, resting against the wall, was a tall silver fridge. Three black and durable guitar cases sat beside the fridge. One of the guitars was decorated with Castle Vania stickers, one was unadorned, and the other had stickers of the planets. Tech equipment surrounded the area. Centered in the lounging area sat a proud leather couch in the shape of a "C". On the low wooden table, in front of the couch, was a blue tinted bong and some weed paraphernalia. A cool, navy blue rug in the lounging area separated the space.

Lorenzo took pride in the fact that this space was accessible to him. He first saw Ray, the lead singer. He was lounging on the leather couch with his girlfriend Page, the lead guitarist. Lorenzo appreciated that they were an attractive couple. Both had pleasing symmetrical faces and disciplined bodies. As usual, they wore matching outfits-a black tank top and black jeans. They were almost invisible while sitting on the black leather couch. However, the disco ball lights danced over every surface.

Ray noticed Lorenzo, then the massive wall of light behind him and said, "Yo what's up, Lo?" His voice was silky smooth. "What time is it? Why is it so bright outside?"

Before Lorenzo could respond to Ray's question, Page began to violently cough. In quick response, Lorenzo walked to the tall silver fridge. As he went deeper into the garage, the dank smell of weed became stronger. Ignoring this, Lorenzo opened the fridge and retrieved a yellow, no name box of apple juice.

Ray took the drink for Page and said, "Much appreciated."

With the straw, Ray punctured the opening of the juice box and offered the prepared drink to Page. Her coughing fit subsided, and she sipped the sweet liquid. Apparent relief was displayed on her face.

Lorenzo removed his school bag from his back and placed it on the rug in front of him. He joined the couple on the couch and said, "That's what heroes are for." *That definitely sounded cool,* Lorenzo thought sarcastically.

Ray ignored Lorenzo's comment and said, "That's the face she wears when we have sex."

In response, Page slapped Ray's arm.

"YO! Ow!"

Suddenly, the door at the back of the garage opened. The Zhang twins stepped into their garage.

"Yo, sup, Lo," said Dylan Zhang.

"Sup, Lo," said Deckard Zhang.

Dylan and Deckard were identical twins. Dylan, the bass player, had a wicked black mohawk and wore a green Weezer t-shirt. He paired this with long black basketball shorts. Deckard, the drummer, had a black crew cut and wore a plain blue shirt. He parried this with comfortable khaki shorts.

Lorenzo made the peace sign and said, "Sup D's."
"I can smell that you guys started without us," commented Deckard. His voice was extremely deep.

"I know a quick remedy," said Dylan. Unlike his twin, puberty had made Dylan's voice fair and easy to listen to. Because of this Page nominated him to be a backup singer, supporting Ray's vocals. The rest of the band agreed however his confidence was not yet there.
The twins sat down beside Lorenzo. One on either side of him. From the blue tinted bong, Dylan prepared a toke.

After preparing a bowl of marijuana, Dylan winked and offered it to his brother. He said, "Wisdom before beauty."

Gratefully, Deckard took the bong. Page cut in, "You know Dylan, you just called yourself stupid." Page reached into her pocket and tossed Dylan the lighter. "You'll need this, stupid." Dylan caught it and passed it over to his brother.

Dylan glared and said, "Having beauty means being stupid? Since when?" Unbothered, Deckard lit his toke and breathed deep. Lorenzo watched as the lighter flame was pulled towards the prepared green herb. The flame took and through the blue tinted glass he could see smoke, and bubbling water.

"Never mind that," said Page. "How are the lyric's coming along, Lo'?"
Ray perked up. Their last song, written by Lorenzo, was a local success. Lorenzo watched Deckard finish his toke in one breath. He blew the smoke toward the open garage door. The dank smell of weed filled the space. It smelled citrusy.

By way of answer, Lorenzo reached to his bag at his feet. He opened it and got his notebook out. At the same time, by way of remote, closed the massive garage door.

"Smarrt keep that good-good in," said Deckard.

"The lyrics are coming along swimmingly," said Lorenzo in a pleased voice. He flipped through his notebook's pages. The dancing lights illuminated his sketches and lyrics.
"Tight," said Ray. "I'm excited to see what our ghostwriter came up with." He then placed a hand on Page's thigh.

Lorenzo saw this and coughed.

"Um, ye," responded Lorenzo. "I should be done by tomorrow. I can show you guys at SuperCrawl."

"Dooope," said Deckard. Although he was seated right beside Lorenzo, Deckard's voice sounded faraway.

Lorenzo felt Dylan's warm hand on his shoulder. "Good shit Lo," he said. "Knew we could count on you."

Abruptly, Ray and Page got up from the couch.

"Woah. Where the hell are you guys going?" Questioned Dylan.

"We're gonna go fulfill our carnal cravings," he said. His voice was full of gladness. "We'll be back in a bit. Keep the virgin here, company."

Page laughed softly and, by the hand, led Ray to the door the Zhang twins had just entered from. Before the attractive couple disappeared, Lorenzo saw Ray wink at him.

"You know what that means," said Deckard solemnly.

"They get to slam, and we get to jam!" answered Dylan.
The twins fist bumped and, in unison, got up from the sofa. They moved to the band practice area. As the D's prepared their instruments, Lorenzo put his notebook down and retrieved the cell phone from his pocket.

The tuning of a bass guitar filled the garage space. Lorenzo opened his phone and tapped a blue application. This opened a picture. He saw a girl sitting up on a bed. Her lower half was under the covers but her pink lace bra and agreeable face was shown. Additionally, she wore a smug expression. He began to type out a message.

...

Back in Sophia Reeves' room, atop her desk, her emerald cell phone vibrated softly. Tipsy Pixie's FairySnap account had received a direct message from Lil' Lion.

SUPERCRAWL

You can't spell fart without art. - A

"Did the Ericson's square up and leave?" asked Carmine Cavallone.

Carmine was standing in the kitchen with his hands on his hips. He had just finished putting the vegetables back into the storage room. His question was directed at Arianna Cavallone, who had just entered the kitchen from the dining room door. In response, she chose to let her husband's question hang in the air.

Arianna had become accustomed to the kitchen aroma. The fragrant smell of fresh tomato sauce permeated the space. She noticed that her husband's chefs' outfit was stained by tomato sauce. His white sleeves were rolled up to the elbow and there was a pink line on his left shoulder. She wondered how Carmine managed to spill sauce on himself like that.

Her hair was tied up into a graceful brown bun. A pencil pierced its center. She wore her typical black work dress. Carmine appreciated that this dress accentuated her soft curves while not being overtly sexual.

Coldly, Arianna's dark brown eyes observed that Carmine had finished putting the leftover ingredients away and that her son was standing by the large steel skin. Lorenzo was currently scraping a large pan clean. The faucet was left on and running water could be heard.

Swiftly, Liam Cavallone entered the kitchen and announced, "The Ericson's have just left the building." He stood in front of the kitchen table right beside his mom.

It was eight p.m. and the Cavallone family restaurant closed its doors in record time.

"Wonderful," said Carmine. He looked at Arianna. "Would you

please lock up the place?" Carmine asked. "I'll go get dressed for our appointment."

Lorenzo turned off the faucet. The sound of running water was cut off. He turned around to face his family. Lorenzo saw his brother remove the apron around his waist.

"But of course," Arianna formally replied.

Her mind was on the upcoming appointment. It would be the first meeting with their divorcee mediator. She anticipated that this conference would be unpleasant and disagreeable. In order to distract herself, Arianna locked eyes with Lorenzo.

"You boys have fun at SuperCrawl tonight," she said. Her voice was now full of tenderness and care. Arianna reached up with her right hand and softly ruffled the hair on Liam's' head. "And no monkey business!" With those last words, she pirouetted on her heels and exited the kitchen through the same door Liam had entered.

"We'll probably be sleeping by the time you get home," said Carmine. He adjusted his thin framed glasses and checked his silver watch. "So, I don't need to remind you to bring your house keys and come in quietly." Carmine retrieved his wallet from his pocket. "Here's some money. Enjoy yourselves tonight."

Liam took the twenty-dollar bill from his dad and with a soft smile said, "Thanks old man."

Lorenzo dried his hands off on a towel and stepped closer to his father. He leaned into his dad, wrapped his right arm around him and with a full smile said, "Thanks, Dad!"

In response, Carmine wrapped an arm around his son and embraced him. "Don't mention it," said Carmine. Lorenzo seized the offered twenty- dollar bill. They detached from one another. Carmine wiped his hands off on a towel and exited the kitchen.

"Let's go get ready," Liam said. "We got thirty minutes before Bruce is here." Lorenzo nodded and presented his brother with his right thumb pointed up. They had discussed the plan earlier.

...

Four hours ago, Lorenzo and Liam were in their rooms getting dressed. Both their doors were left open.

"So, Bruce is coming by with some soccer buddies at 8:30ish," said Liam. He projected his voice so that it could be heard across the hallway. He did this in the same manner that he projected his voice across the soccer field.

Lorenzo was buttoning up his shirt when he said, "Sounds good!" He grabbed his cell phone off his desk and turned it on. His eyebrows raised when he saw the time. "It's already 4:03! I'm heading down!" He called out.

"I'll be down in a hot sec," returned Liam.

...

At 8:27 p.m. Lorenzo and Liam stood at the back exit of the restaurant.

"We're off!" called out the Cavallone brothers.

For tonight's adventure Lorenzo planned out his outfit with care; his black zip-up sweater was left open, it revealed the image of a hydra from his favourite band T-shirt. Around his neck, underneath his shirt, Lorenzo wore a simple silver chain. Tight black jeans with plain black vans completed Lorenzo's getup.

Liam, on the other hand, did not put much thought into his choice of clothing. He wore his snug navy blue, high school soccer team hoodie. He matched this with dark blue sweat shorts and wore puma ankle socks with adidas flip-flops on his feet. Comfort was the only motivation for tonight's outfit.

"Stay safe!" called out Carmine from somewhere in the restaurant.

The restaurant's back door closed with a solid thud. Outside, Lorenzo pulled on the metal handle to ensure that it locked. "We good," said Lorenzo.

"Perfect," said Liam. "Bruce just texted me that he's out front."

Although it was a pleasant evening the hot smell of garbage entered the noses of the brothers. Familiarity with the revolting smell allowed the boys a type of immunity. Liam saw that the dumpster at the rear of the restaurant had been left open.

"What are you going to spend your money on?" Lorenzo asked.

Liam walked over to the dumpster, closed the heavy plastic lid, and made sure to lock it closed. He then said, "A beanie or some food. I heard the food trucks last year were nuts." Liam dusted his off hands and applied some hand sanitizer. "What about you?"

"I'd spend it on getting our parents back together," said Lorenzo sadly.

Liam stopped and looked at his brother. "Lorenzo," his voice became serious, "that's their decision."

"You can't be okay with this."

"Would you be okay suffering in a relationship you didn't want to be in?"

Liam's pertinent question forced Lorenzo to pause and reflect. After a brief moment Lorenzo admits that he's never been in a relationship.

"Well then," says Lorenzo, "there you go. Come on; they should be out front."

Lorenzo and Liam turned the corner and saw Bruce's black Dodge
Caravan. The car was still running. Silently, Liam walked to the side door. He winked at Lorenzo and opened the van door swiftly.

"AHHHH!" He forcefully roared.

Genuine screams were heard in immediate reply. Lorenzo, on the other hand, could not contain his mirth. He laughed pleasantly.

"You absolute demon!" accused Bruce from the driver seat. His fellow riders shared an equally reproachful expression. "I thought you were coach Armstrong!'

Liam held his stomach in elation and there were tears of joy in his eyes.
He was proud that his jump scare worked so well. His contagious laugh helped settle down the occupants in the van. They looked defeated but energized. Liam recognized Jamie Hawthorn and gave him a head nod.

"Get in you schmucks!" said Jaime.

He wore a grey plaid shirt and sharp blue jeans, and fist bumped Liam and Lorenzo as they entered the van. The Cavallone brothers sat in the back seats.

The smell of the van pleased Lorenzo. It smelled of fresh pine. Liam, on the other hand, recalled the last time he was in this van. It had smelt of body odor and sweaty soccer gear. He too was pleased about the current smell.

"Yo, where is Raza?" questioned Liam. "Don't tell me he flaked again."

"Why'd you ask if you already knew?" answered Bruce from the driver seat.

Bruce was wearing the same snug navy-blue high school soccer hoodie that Liam wore with light blue jeans. Beside him, in the passenger seat, sat his older sister.

"I asked because I hoped I was wrong," said Liam. He tried not to allow the disappointment to enter his voice. "Well whatever. It's nice to see you again Penelope. Oh yeah, Penelope, this is my younger brother Lorenzo and Lorenzo this is Bruce's older sister Penelope."

From the backseat, Lorenzo observed Penelope. She was a small girl but appeared mature. Her natural brown curly hair orbited her head. He thought if he pressed his hand against her hair his hand would bounce back. Penelope wore a stylish tan jacket over a simple black hoodie, parried with black jeans. Nike running shoes covered her feet.

"Sup Liam and nice to meet you Lorenzo," Penelope said. Her

voice wasb as sweet as honey. "You know, I've heard about you, Lorenzo. Our English teacher read your poems to our class."

"Yes, yes the Cavallone family name is known throughout the land," said Lorenzo in a sarcastically pretentious tone.

Liam smiled and softly punched his brother's arm. The contact made Lorenzo crack a smile.

"Yup," said Bruce. "The captain and the poet. I am honored that the Cavallone brothers will ride in my humble carriage."

"Yo, why the fuck are we still parked here?" cut in Jamie.

"So eloquently put," replied Penelope.

With a smile Bruce rolled his eyes.

"Onward Mr.Bigby! Let's proceed to tonight's entertainment!" said Lorenzo.

Bruce stepped on the gas and said, "Cavallone commands!"

...

Super Crawl focuses on promoting local talent. And so, this year's summer celebration attracted a plethora of individuals. People flooded the downtown street. Like the previous year, Super Crawl was divided into three simple sectors. The chief attraction was the main stage. Here, local bands entertained the crowd. The city would even book a headliner to close out the night. This year they got Lights. The second sector is reserved for the local merchants. Artists, woodworkers, glassblowers and even clothiers promoted their goods. It is known that these vendors are required to fill out forms a year in advance to get a booth and license to sell. Thus, the merchants fiercely compete with one another. Intense bartering, yelling matches and physical fights were common in this sector. The last sector is where the group is now, in the mobile food court.

In front of the group was a vehicle imitating a large crab. It was painted bright orange and had opposable claws. The smell of crab poutine made Penelope's mouth water. Beside the metal crustacean was a plain black food truck that specializes in hot dogs. Lorenzo was suddenly aware of the many people around him consuming these hot dogs. He decided they looked delicious. Bruce eyed one with evident envy.

On the crustacean's left, towards the vendor's portion of the festival, was a puffed-up truck. It had been decorated in a way that made the automobile appear deep fried. Liam and Jamie were currently studying its chalk menu. They were astonished to discover that this truck would deep fry pickles and ice crème. Lorenzo's ears could distinguish live music above the conversations.

"What have we decided?" asked Liam to the group.

"I have decided to leave," said Lorenzo. The group turned inward to face the youngest Cavallone. "I'm going to meet up with some friends. Thanks for the ride and peace out." He fist bumped everyone before leaving the group.

As Liam's fist made contact with his brother's he said, "Text me if you need anything."

Lorenzo winked and made the peace sign in response. Liam watched his brother's back as he headed down the street toward the merchant section.

Suddenly, Penelope pointed her right index finger towards the crab truck. "My stomach has decided crab!" she announced loudly.

"Well, your stomach is going to have to wait," said Bruce. "I forgot my wallet in the car."

Penelope's proud stance was instantly deflated.

Jamie frantically searched his body with his hands. After some hard pats he said, "I hope I left mine there too."

"You two would forget your head if it wasn't attached to your body," said Liam. "You guys go get your money and Penelope and I can wait here."

"Sounds like a plan," answered Penelope.

"Back in a flash," said Jamie.

The two boys left Liam and Penelope in the middle of the street and threaded their way through the thick crowd on their way back to the van. After some silence Penelope turned to Liam and said, "So, uh, I don't mean to bring it up but uh Bruce told me about your parents. Do you want to talk about it? How you holding up?"

Liam sneezed.

"Bless you," offered Penelope.

"Thanks. And I'm okay, thanks for asking," said Liam. "I think, I'm holding it together." With a sudden swiftness he was touched with a melancholy feeling. Compelled to let it out he said, "People say it's easy to love. You simply fall into it. But my parents are falling out of love...so I'm kind of confused."

Penelope's head turned from the crab food truck to look at Liam's face. She heard the sincerity in his voice and saw his somber look.

"Love is a tough topic," Penelope said. "But I do know It's okay to be confused. In fact, I'd say it's a requirement in the process."

Liam saw that she was about to say more but quickly closed her mouth. Penelope turned around and with her eyes searched the alleyway behind them. Curiously, Liam followed her attention. He saw groups of people criss-cross in front of a dark alleyway.

"Did you hear that?" asked Penelope.

"Hear what?" asked Liam.

Penelope scowled and said, "Follow me."

Liam watched as her tan jacket cut through the crowd of people. Liam followed her. He stepped to the lip of the alleyway. Liam's eyes squinted to pierce the dark shadows.

"Oi! Penelope! Where'd you go?" he called out.

No one behind Liam paid any attention. He continued walking into the alleyway. His foot kicked something. Liam looked down and saw that he had struck a metal garbage can lid. His left big toe stung.

"Liam over here!" called out an excited voice. "Look what I found!"

Ignoring the pain, Liam stepped over the lid and, with fresh awareness, followed the sound of the voice. "Ugh," said Liam. The rank smell of garbage had entered his nose and the sour smell of urine lingered in the alleyway air. In a few more steps he found Penelope crouched behind a dark green dumpster, like the one he closed earlier.

"What kind of garbage did you find?" questioned Liam.

Penelope turned around. "You know, it's not all garbage in this city," she answered. Liam could now see a small grey ball of fur in her arms.

"Huh?" produced Liam.

"Look," said Penelope. She stood and moved into the streetlight. Liam followed her and looked at what Penelope was carrying. His eyebrows raised immediately. Liam saw a tiny grey kitten in her hands.

"Yo!" called out Jamie from the lip of the alleyway. He stood there along with Bruce.

"What's Penelope up to now?" yelled Bruce in a tone Penelope was accustomed to.

...

By this time Lorenzo had made it to the main stage. He stood at the back of the crowd. He witnessed the cover band play some Red-Hot Chili Peppers. He could not recall the songs name; however, he noticed the crowd was singing and dancing along with approval. Lorenzo's head swiveled left and right. He couldn't find any of the Snake Detection Hypothesis band members. He saw someone with a mohawk, and hope was ignited in his heart. Unfortunately, he realized the cool mohawk was attached to a lady. It did not belong to Dylan Zhang.

Saddened, Lorenzo turned around and walked up some steps. The flight of stairs led him to a spot above the festivities. A small crowd of people lingered near the top smoking cigarettes. Lorenzo passed by them all and called Ray on his cell phone. After three rings Ray answered.

"Yo, Lo'! How's it hanging?" said Ray.

"I'm chilling at SuperCrawl," answered Lorenzo. "Where are you guys?"

"Yeah, I told Deckard to text you. I guess he forgot. We uh bailed on SuperCrawl. Page got us a gig at the Judge. We're on in fifteen."

Lorenzo swallowed and said, "That's dope! I'll show you the lyrics whenever. Have a killer set!"

"Ay thanks, Lo'. Rock on, bro," answered Ray.

Lorenzo hung up the call and lifted his head. He recognized where he was. Lorenzo stood on the second floor of the downtown mall. He was still outside but he could see an entrance into the mall just ahead of him. His reflection glared back at him from the buildings' window.

After three minutes of staring at himself, Lorenzo had come to a decision. He opened his cell phone. He tapped a blue application and began typing a message. The contents of this message are private, but it basically inquired about the likelihood of receiving physical intimacy from the receiver. After Lorenzo hit send, he released a weighty sigh.

...

Back in Sophia's Reeves' room, atop her desk beside the mechanical fan, her emerald cell phone softly vibrated. Tipsy Pixie's FairySnap account had just received a direct message from Lil' Lion.

Lorenzo's Flashback

One. Two. Three. Flash!

Black and white.

What an enticing opening, eh!? Where is it all heading?

Command some patience please and let us dive into the memory of Lorenzo Cavallone. Into his most cherished memory.

...

It was the ten-year year anniversary of the Hawk and Sparrow. The small, local coffee shop decided to rejoice in a public fashion. For celebration the Hawk and Sparrow opened its doors to the locals, musicians, poets, and scholars were personally invited to the event. And so, over the course of the day, bands played, conversations flowed, congratulations were received, coffee was sipped, and pastries were devoured.

On that day, this simple coffee shop could not contain its celebration. Many people had spilled outside to accommodate the crowd already inside. In fact, police were made aware of the event and kept a patrolling surveillance unit in the area to ensure the peace was maintained. The quaint coffee shop was the very picture of celebration.

The Cavallone family was present during this matter. Carmine Cavallone's parents had enjoyed doing business with the owners of the Hawk and Sparrow. The good business continued with the son. The family had accepted the email invitation and were presently waiting for Lorenzo to take the stage.

Lorenzo Cavallone had entered his name in the closing event. In celebration of their ten years, The Hawk and Sparrow held a slam poetry contest. Despite the small size of the coffee shop, the prize of the contest was massive. It had been funded by the loyal patrons of the shop. Thus, the winning prize was a week-long trip to Costa Rica with a consolation prize of becoming the only V.I.P customer for a year.

Lorenzo was chosen as the first to perform his material. As he stood to the side of the stage, his hands were slick with sweat, so he wiped them on his jeans. To distract himself, he looked out the front window. There, he witnessed a man bump into a woman, forcing her to drop her drink. His attention returned inside and focused on the low hushing that came with the sudden stopping of conversation. Something was happening.

From the back of the coffee shop, near the payment counter, the Cavallone family saw the M.C take the stage.

"Testing. One, two, three," came the clear amplified voice of the woman speaking on stage. The rest of the chatting stopped. "Good evening, everyone!" the charismatic M.C began. "How are we feeling tonight?" Rowdy cheers were heard in response. "I wouldn't have it any other way. I have the honor of being your M.C this evening. And that privilege comes with one rule to announce. From now on we will be snapping for applause. This is a classy place, holding a classy contest. That means snaps only for the slam poetry contest. Capeesh?" This was met with a chorus of snapping. "Spectacular!" commented the M.C. "Now, let's get this slam poetry contest moving! Our first contestant is an elementary school student who has a burning passion for poetry. Please help me welcome Lorenzo Cavallone to the stage."

Lorenzo couldn't recall where he found the courage to walk towards the M.C, shake her hand and take the offered mic, nevertheless, that's exactly what he did. There he stood at the center of attention. Lorenzo distinctly remembers searching through the faces in the crowd and finding his family's proud smiles and raised thumbs. This sight gave him a mountain of courage.

"Ahem," his high-pitched voice started. "Hey everyone, my, um, name is Lorenzo Cavallone, and I will now recite three original poems." He took a deep breath to stabilize himself, cleared his throat, exhaled sharply, and then began,

Sisyphus' instrument: is the bolder.

She wouldn't listen, But I told her.

Sisyphus' curse: is not getting older.

He was warm,

But it's getting colder.

Sisyphus' crime: cheating death twice.

Look above,

That's the price.

Lorenzo received scattered, but enthusiastic snaps from the audience. Embolden from what he had just accomplished, Lorenzo moved on to his next poem.

Small flies buzz by the spider queen.

Strength and grace distract from what it means.

Pleasures in screams, purposes in dreams.

Deep down she craves,

Her heartbeat raves.

Pleasures in screens, purposes in creams.

Web of lies made of silk, eyes for guys made of milk.

Pleasures of the harp pierce so sharp.

Additional snapping was offered in response. Lorenzo took three sharp breaths before he began his last poem.

In Hades kingdom of Decay,

Lies Cerberus,

The Three that must sit and stay.

Lies Persephone,

Six months did the graceful goddess pay.

A place with no lyre,

Yet a river of flaming fire.

Elysium the paradise of salvation,

Cut by the river of lamentation.

Jewels Hades kicks,

Into the deep water of the murky Styx.

A wild torrent of snaps came from the audience. From the back, Arianna put two fingers in her mouth and breathed out a piercing whistle. Carmine stood in astonished disbelief and Liam could not have been prouder of his younger brother.

Standing on stage, Lorenzo experienced elation. He couldn't feel the top of his head. The clear signs of approval from the cheerful patrons brought waves of satisfaction he couldn't fully comprehend or understand.

…

Lorenzo Cavallone's flashback finishes here. But, in the name of curiosity, I will fill you in on the gloomy outcome of the contest. Unfortunately for many, the contest was rigged from the start. The patrons who funded the magnificent prize had concocted a deal. The contestant who they chose would possess the judge's favor. And so, like many contests, large or small, the winners won beforehand. Although, it must be stated that Lorenzo's poems were remembered vividly by the patrons in attendance and so while not winning his words were retained.

Act III: S U N D A Y

DARK
WINGS

"God created death to rein on life." - A

It was raining outside. A calming constant drizzle. Raza Singh ignored the wet weather in the comfort of his lavish bedroom. He was seated at his ornate desk reviewing his statistic's textbook. To help him focus on his laptop, he played The Story So Far lo-fi album that Sophia Reeves recommended.

Raza's room was immaculate. All his clothes were folded and put away, stowed in the tough mahogany chest drawer against the wall. The closet space, at the back of the room, was organized like a library catalogue. The most used item, Raza's soccer equipment, was placed on the floor of the closet clean and ready to be used. Additionally, the twin bed at the corner of the room was neat and tidy. It was freshly prepared by Raza before he began his homework. The soft extravagant purple comforter appeared convivial. An old cat would find trouble resisting the desire to rest on such a finely made bed. The rain on the window, in front of Raza's tough ornate desk, was the only picture of chaos that could be found.

Raza's eyes followed his right index finger as it scanned through the detailed graph within the textbook. He scratched the back of his head and observed the time on his laptop which displayed 12:03 P.M. *I've been studying for two hours now,* Raza thought.

Suddenly, over the chill music, Raza heard a knock at his door. After another knock Kunal Singh entered the room. He turned to looked at his father. Kunal was wearing a maroon dress shirt with black slacks. He also wore a jovial expression.

"Ha Ha! This sight brings joy to my heart," said Kunal. "To find my son studying so dutifully. It reminds me of myself! But come. You deserve a break from such discipline. Your mother has prepared a light meal. Come enjoy her delicious cooking."

Raza was delighted to hear his father's news. Hunger had been nagging at him over the past half hour.

"Count me in!" answered Raza.

He paused the YouTube video, stood up from his desk and followed his father out of his room.

In the dining room, Jiya Singh placed the delicious lunch on the gorgeous table. Raza's eyes locked onto the fresh falafels with rice and sauce. He smiled instantly. Kunal placed a hand on the back of his son's shoulder to prod him farther into the dining room.

It was a tasteful space. The Singh dining room contained a graceful ambiance. A gold and white color scheme gave the area a pious look. A master crafted oak table with gold lining sat in the middle of the room. Fancy black leather chairs with white lining surrounded the custom table. The focal point of the room, the opulent chandelier, hung high above. Its dangling radiance illuminated the room in soft welcoming light. Ever since he was a child Raza thought the chandelier looked like a large sunny jelly fish.

Once they were all seated Raza said, "Thank you mother, for this meal. I was feeling famished."

Jiya smiled knowingly and said, "You are most welcomed, my beloved Raza. Please dig in."

Kunal and Jiya joined hands as their son placed portions of food on a luxurious plate.

"This gloomy weather means nothing when our family can be warm and eat to our fill," commented Kunal.

"Indeed," said Jiya. "We are indifferent to the cold rain when we live in such a warm home." Before Kunal or Jiya began to eat they shared a meaningful glance.

"You know," began Kunal. "Raza, that because we work at McMaster you will receive the privilege of commuting with us. We could probably hang out and chill on certain days when our schedules line up."

"How fun," added Jiya.

Raza swallowed a mouth full of food and said, "I haven't been accepted yet, but I *can't wait* for the opportunity to spend even more time with both of you."

Jiya's sensitive ear heard the slight tone of sarcasm and said, "You'd be ignorant and wasteful to neglect such opportunities."

"Hmmm," sounded Kunal. He cleared his throat and looked to his son. Kunal was committed to tell him a secret he hoped would instill caution.

"Now, Raza, I have some dark news to tell you," Kunal began. He waited for Raza's undivided attention. Raza's curiosity was piqued. His father rarely began topics of conversation in this manner. "Last week there was a report of a suicide on campus."

Raza's eyebrows raised instinctively. This wasn't the first time he had heard this happening, but it was equally startling. In fact, a past soccer teammate dropped out of a season because his best friend had committed suicide. He looked to his mother. Jiya's hand covered her mouth, and she was looking down toward her untouched plate of food.

Kunal let out a sigh. "I hope I did not ruin your appetite," he said. "It would be a shame to waste your mothers' delicious meal. However, if I did, I did it in the name of awareness…or rather attention! Your mother and I would like you to be attentive of suicide and the devastating doom it brings."

Jiya could not contain herself any longer and said, "University life can become stressful for students. Overbearing. Even so, you must not ever flirt with hopelessness, Raza. Do you understand?"

Raza heard the testing note of the question. He also heard the repulsive motherly love in her voice.

"I understand," said Raza, "I promise."

SUNDAY
STEALING

Good people set the record straight. -A

The first thing Lorenzo Cavallone noticed was the rain. From the comfort of his warm bed, Lorenzo observed the window in his room. His eyes watched a small drop of wetness. He thought it moved like a worm made of water. Gravity had been pulling it down, from the top of the window plane, for the last thirty-three seconds. Like the weather, he was in a melancholy mood.

Unmotivated to move, Lorenzo drifted back to sleep. Quickly he fell into a vivid dream. Lorenzo dreamt that he was at the base of an erupting volcano. Ash covered the sky and mesmerizing magma made its way down the sides of the great mountain. Lorenzo found that he was untroubled by the cloudy ash or the insanely hot lava. Also, he felt a supreme desire to climb up the erupting volcano. To stand at its apex. So, Lorenzo walked up and through a trail of lava. Halfway up the erupting volcano Lorenzo focused his sight at its peak. There, at the top, emanating through the dark and ashy sky, stood a glowing woman with wings extended. The ultimate awe of such a sight caused Lorenzo to slip. Suddenly, and painfully his imperviousness to the heat and ash were removed. He began coughing violently and his feet and legs began to itch with pure agony. The tremendous pain caused Lorenzo to fall to his knees. Unsure of what to do he put his hands together in prayer. The woman at the top watched with indifference.

Abruptly, Lorenzo awoke. His bed sheets were wet with worry. Lorenzo removed his covers and caught his breath. After a few moments he searched the window with his eyes. Looking for change Lorenzo found it was the same outside. It was still raining.

Pursued by the pressure to pee and the desire to shower, Lorenzo hurried out of his room and entered the washroom. There he sniffed a couple times like a dog. He identified the smell of lavender. It was coming from the purple candle on the sink counter. After quickly pissing and showering, Lorenzo wet index finger and thumb to extinguish the candle's flame. It went out with a hiss. At the same time Lorenzo's stomach grumbled loudly.

"Alright," he said to his stomach.

Instead of going back to his room, Lorenzo made his way downstairs. Animal hunger motivated his actions. While at the top of the stairs, with his hands, he reached up high to stretch out. As he passed the bar, he touched the faux 2006 Italian FIFA world cup champions trophy and then stopped in front of the kitchen doors.

Looking through the window on the beige kitchen door, Lorenzo saw his older brother preparing a meal. From behind the door, Lorenzo's sensitive nose told him he was making a grilled cheese sandwich. *With maybe some soup?* Lorenzo thought. He turned back around and observed the family restaurant dining space. Everything was as he expected.

The family restaurant was closed today because his parents were at another appointment with the divorce mediator. Open and honest discussions about their relationship were taking longer than anticipated. Already, this was the Cavallone's third session.

Lorenzo knew if he was going to strike it must be now. He tip-toed to the bar. Once behind the modest bar he ignored everything but the old cash register. It was in its usual spot. Under the counter beside the old Canada day napkins. The family kept the traditional device to store petty cash. Unexpectedly, Lorenzo heard a pan fall in the kitchen and, like a hunted animal, instantly froze. He waited five heartbeats before moving again.

His cold hands reached down to the lower shelf where the old register sat. Arianna had showed him and his brother how to use the outdated device long ago. He applied this knowledge now. Lorenzo opened the old register with the pull of a lever. It opened with a metal click. Quickly, Lorenzo removed $500 in $50s and $20s then closed the machine.

Lorenzo stuffed the cash in his right-hand pocket and made his way into the kitchen.

"Caught red handed!" said Liam Cavallone.

For the second time today, Lorenzo froze. Liam pointed a broken handle to a handless pan in the kitchen skin. Lorenzo's shoulders relaxed.

"However, its noble sacrifice gave us food," said Liam.

And as if he was a magician, Liam presented a plate of two yummy grilled cheese sandwiches.

"Thanks, bro," said Lorenzo with a smile. "I'm starving and mad thirsty."

COFFEE
CUP

If you require profits, one must rule. - A

In the Reeves apartment there was a noise of pure pleasure.

"Mmmm!" blissfully sounded Sophia once again.

"Sophia! The sounds you make suggest Gordan Ramsey cooked this longanisa and rice," said Marge Reeves playfully.

...

The two ladies sat in their humble apartment kitchen. They sat at a simple round wooden table in matching wooden chairs. The space was warm and smelled sweet. Behind the ladies sat the prehistoric yellowish apartment stove. It was currently cooling down from use and the equally old beige fridge hummed with a constant current. While their kitchen lacked space, it contained a calm peace.

On this rainy afternoon Sophia felt fresh. She had just taken a shower and so, her damp dark brown hair hung loosely about her shoulders. Her mother had told her to comb her hair just before she had starting eating. Sophia answered her with a casual "I will later mom." She wore a tight grey tank top and baggy grey sweat pants.

Sophia's mother, on the other hand, felt rather gloomy. Her sweet sleep had been robbed by a phone call. Her manager informed her extremely early that she was needed to fill in for a sick call. Marge accepted the call of duty. Quite regretfully so because she had a second date with a gentleman planned for today. However, today's constant rain meant the date was cancelled. The plan had been to enjoy an afternoon coffee at the Hawk and Sparrow and then enjoy a pleasant walk at the nearby park.

Despite her gloom, Marge felt a little better after seeing her daughter consume her food so enthusiastically. She was already dressed for work. Marge wore her blue spring uniform with her matching blue HSR baseball cap.

...

In response to her mother's playful comment Sophia opened her mouth to display the mushed-up food in her mouth.

Before she could speak with her mouth full, Marge got up from the table and said, "Wow! Truly such ladylike behavior! It's no wonder you're still single."

This comment genuinely wrinkled Sophia's playful mood. Marge continued towards the door of the apartment and put on her blue HSR rain jacket on.

Sophia swallowed her food and said, "Make sure you bring an umbrella. We wouldn't want the wicked witch of the West to melt from the rainwater."

"Ha!" responded Marge, as she put on her rain boots. She used the nice shoehorn Sophia had purchased her on her last birthday. "I'm still surprised my wicked offspring survived a shower." Marge opened the door of the apartment. "I'll be back later tonight, text me if you need anything. Comb your hair back and I love you."

Still seated at the table, Sophia rolled her eyes and said, "Drive safe, I love you too!"

The door locked shut and Sophia was left alone in the apartment with half a plate of food. Before finishing her meal, she removed her emerald cell phone from her pocket to observe the time. Her hazel eyes ignored the notifications and saw it was 1:01 p.m. Right after her meal, Sophia was going to respond to all the notifications she received last night.

To motivate herself Sophia unlocked her phone and pressed the music application. She then clicked shuffle on one of the playlists she had created. From her emerald cell phone "Doves in the Wind" by SZA began to play. Only then did Sophia place her device face down on the simple table and finish her plate.

...

Three hours later the weather got worse. The soft rain turned into a torrential downpour. On the downtown road, Marge noticed that drivers were driving with extra caution. Her bus was empty, but with renewed determination she adjusted her hat and pushed slowly through the intersection.

Marge was minutes away from the downtown bus station. This was the point of her route where it would end and then, once again, repeat. She planned on staying at the station for five minutes. A nice respite from the constant, heavy rain, and the other drivers.

It's raining cats and dogs today, thought Marge. *I could be piloting a submarine right 'bout now.*

Carefully, Marge changed lanes. Through the rain and wipers, she saw the bus station. She was turning into the bus station when a bright blue blur cut in front of her path. Instinctively, she stomped on the brakes.

"Fucksakes!" said Marge. "Is that a person!?"

The bus came to an abrupt stop. Marge's seatbelt kept her from experiencing harsh whiplash. While motionless, the sound of the bus engine was drowned out by the bombardment of rain. It was as if Marge was inside a rain stick. Unexpectedly, a vehicle hit the back of her bus and, unfortunately, the seatbelt could not fully impede the incoming force. Violently, Marge's head and neck was thrown forward, and then backward.

When her eyes cleared of the white flashes, she looked out the window. Although Marge was not one hundred percent sure, she thought she had seen a man on a bike cut into an alleyway. Instinctively, her mind thought of Zeke.

Employees from the bus station heard the collision and ran over to assist. The manager who had called Marge in this morning knocked on the front door of the bus.

"Is everyone okay?" asked Richard McPherson. His loud voice cut through the simple bus door as well as Marge's confusion.

"It's just me and I'm good," responded Marge. With the click of a button she opened the door and presented him with a thumbs up. Unsure if he had heard it the first time, she then repeated her message again.

Under a large dark blue umbrella stood Richard McPherson. The tall figure stood outside the open door. He wore a similar outfit to Marge's. Although the accident was problematic, they were both happy to know no one else was on the bus.

"Okay, sit tight," said Richard. "I'm going to go check on the other driver."

"Sounds good," replied Marge.

While her manager was checking on the other driver, Marge checked herself. She moved her arms without strain and her legs responded with ease. The back of her neck felt sore. With her hands, Marge massaged her neck.

"Are you okay?" called out a paramedic from outside the open bus door. Her voice was thick with concern. Marge turned her neck slowly to face the new voice. A young female paramedic with thick glasses was standing beside a mature female police officer. The emergency workers stood in the rain with stoic disregard. When they saw Marge give them the thumbs up the officer spoke, "Very good. Are you able to pull into the station?"

"I can manage that," answered Marge.

"Good. For the time being, we have stopped traffic. Please pull into the station now. It is safe," ordered the officer.

As a snail crawls into the safety of a leaf, Marge slowly crept her bus into the station. And there she awaited further instructions.

...

"What's the damage?" asked Richard.

Inside the bus station, in conference room A, sat several individuals. Around a modest oval table, in leather chairs, sat the transit crisis management team and Marge Reeves. Richard had directed his question to the on-call mechanic.

"Bus one is totally *versauen*," answered the old German mechanic in a thick accent. "Bus two is, how-you-say, sal-vage-able." His hair was white, and his hands had thick calloused.

"We've been over this Rolf," said the vice president. "In English please."

"*Kacke kopf*," muttered Rolf.

"I heard that, Rolf!" said Vice President Richard Newport. "I've been studying German. I know what that means. Did you hear that, Michelle?"

"I did not hear a thing vice president," responded the exasperated H.R. representative. "Rolf, why don't you tell us about the buses-"

"In English," interrupted Richard McPherson.

"In English, thank you Richard M," said Michelle. Her tone of voice did not change. "Since you are the mechanic, *the expert,* in this situation."

Rolf twisted the end of his thick white mustache and said, "*Dah*. Bus one is *kaput*. It's no good anymore, *tot*. The rain fried the wiring. Water and electricity are no good. Right, Mr. vice president."

Richard Newport clenched his teeth and said, "Right Rolf. What about Marge's bus? What condition is bus two in?"

"I can save bus two," answered Rolf magnanimously. "We have the spare parts we need for replacement. I can get her fixed by the end of this week." *She was scheduled for a top up in a week anyways haha…shame bus two is totally versauen*, thought Rolf.

"Thank you, Rolf," said Michelle. Her tone of voice changed from fatigued to slightly endearing. "Now, how are the people directly involved? Marge are you okay?"

Marge was seated in the leather office chair at Michelle's immediate left. A yellow trauma blanket was wrapped over her shoulders, and she was fixated on a cup of lukewarm coffee that sat on the table in front of her. *Am I okay?* Marge thought.

"Marge?" prodded Richard M. He snapped his fingers. "Mrs. Reeves?"

"Sorry, I was lost in thought," said Marge. She took a sip of coffee. "Sore neck but I'm good."

"That's a relief," said Michelle. "The paramedics say Bob, the other bus driver, is also good."

"Why did they take him to the hospital then?" asked the vice president.

"I know this one," said Richard M. "I was told they are double checking his vitals, at the hospital, because of his age. Something about making sure he handled the shock properly."

The vice president eyed Rolf. He then nodded his head and said, "Okay, Rolf you're dismissed. Thank you for your services."

"Anytime," said Rolf, "Except when I'm not working, eh."

Once Rolf left conference room A, Richard Newport's shoulders dropped and sighed. He took a sip of his coffee and said, "Through the grace of God, there were no passengers involved. On either bus, means less paperwork for Michelle and I." He cleared his throat. "Your manager, Mr. McPherson, has informed me of your spotless record. An impressive golden record. Nonetheless, Marge Reeve's, you will be fined five hundred dollars for damages. Consider this a slap on the wrist." Richard N. released another sigh. "That's it, keep up your impeccable driving. Today's rain was ungodly, we should be happy this is the extent of the damages."

"Agreed," said Michelle and Richard M.

Marge was only half listening to the conversation. Her attention was still transfixed on the coffee cup in front of her. She thought the white Styrofoam cup looked so sad and utterly alone.

Marge's Flashback

I am saddened to inform you that this will be the last flashback. And so, let us honor this final trip with a deserving embellishment.

On the count of three I will present you with another flash, however, in honor of the occasion, before every number I will present you with a clue to who I am. I hope this idea will whet your appetite.

First, I am known by many epithets. In the spirit of generosity, I will name three. He who is upon his mountain. The dog who swallows millions and the master of secrets.

One.

Second, know that I am, obviously, omnipresent, omniscience and omnipotence.

Two.

Finally, the third clue. Well, this is not truly a clue, it is the motive as to why I was motivated to write this particular drab and utterly vapid story. The reason is thus, I also tire of the pandemic.
Dreadfully so. It is true that during this time I was exceedingly busy, however I still managed to complete many items on my to-do list. Therefore, I was left to face this task.

Three.

Oh, last thing. I nearly neglected to inform you where we will be surveying. Marge Reeves is an adult woman. That means she has a well of memories that dominate her unconscious mind.

Our last flashback will be a trip into her most devastating and demoralizing memory.

Flash.

...

It happened on an early Saturday morning. So early that the sun was moments away from waking up. It occurred on the fifth floor of the same apartment Sophia and Marge Reeves currently live in. It began in the master bedroom.

The room was pitch black. Thick russet curtains were left open revealing a sliding glass door. Through this door one could venture to a constricted balcony area. An area mainly used by Richard Reeves. A place he could smoke his cigarettes. Belmont's were his preferred brand of smokes.

Inside the master bedroom, in the darkness, the Reeves family slept peacefully. The three of them were laying on the king bed with enough room for one more person and a pet. They were all under the cover of a large warm dark blue blanket. The color would match the sea on a cold night. Lamps on the nightstands were turned off. However, above the family, on the ceiling, were glow-in-the dark space stickers. They illuminated the ceiling with a faded radiance.

At 2:57 a.m. Richard slipped out of the warm bed. His exit was not smooth enough to go unnoticed. Marge whispered, "Where are you off to?"

Richard ignored the question and proceeded towards the closet. The lanky man crouched low and collected clothes and a black duffle bag. As he stood the silence in the room was broken. The strap on the bag, when stretched out, let out a nervous squeak.

Although she could not see what made that sound, Marge knew where it came from. In her mind she saw the black duffle bag filled with $25 thousand.

...

The grand amount of money had been obtained on Richard's and Marge's honeymoon. Back then, Marge had pressed the meek Richard to gamble with the money they were given. The marriage money from friends and family. Forced to make a decision, Richard chose to bet on a game he did not truly know how to play. He bet a little more than half of what they were gifted. That money was placed on the green double zero roulette table. In doing so, Richard won an absurd amount of money. $50 thousand.

Half of that amount they had spent on trips, spa days, golf clubs, baby gear, cigarettes, clothing, food, and bills. Eight years later, the rest of the lucky money was in the black duffle bag in the back of the closet. Left there for an intended purpose. On the day they had won the money, after they sobered up from the excitement of winning, Richard and Marge agreed the last half should and would go to their child's post-secondary education.

...

"Dad, can I have a glass of water?" squeaked out Sophia. Her youthful girlish voice came from underneath the covers. She had hidden her face as soon as she detected her father's movements.

"Of course, sweetie," whispered back Richard. His hungry eyes were focused on the dark bag. "I'll be right back."

Sophia's father exited the room with a bundle of clothes and her college money. Once the master bedroom door closed, Marge kissed her daughter's head and began to leave the warm bed. Sophia's small hands gripped her mother's forearm.

"Don't go," whispered Sophia. The sound was barely detectable.

"Don't worry; I'll be right back," promised Marge.

She followed her suspicious husband. As the master bedroom door closed once more, Sophia peeked her small head out from under the covers. Her bright hazel eyes looked up at the ceiling. She focused her sight on the small purple planet she knew to be Pluto.

Outside the master bedroom, Marge, wrapped in a pink robe, saw her husband put on his casual black tennis shoes. He was standing directly ahead of her past the small kitchen and equally petite living room. Marge passed through the kitchen quickly. She did not notice the digital clock and she did not notice that the time read 3:13 a.m. She stopped five feet away from Richard and said, "Where do you think you are going?"

With his shoes on, Richard turned to look at his wife. He stood much taller than her and he held a defiant stance.

Marge steadied herself and glared back at her husband. She saw that he wore a plain black baseball cap, his thick beige jacket zipped up and black cargo pants. On his shoulders he wore the strap of the black duffle bag and on his back was a solid black backpack, which was filled with clothes and accessories.

"I had a bad dream," lied Richard. "I'm going to pay respect for my mom."

"Let-me-get-this-straight," said Marge quickly. "You had a bad dream and so you've decided to take Sophia's money and an extra bag to the King cemetery. All to pay respect…to your dead mom. Am I understanding correctly?" Marge could not help the accusatory tone in her voice.

Richard nonchalantly adjusted the strap on his shoulder and said, "Yeah. You got it."

"Richard," began Marge. Her heart froze with a sudden icy chill. Despite this visceral feeling she continued. "Things aren't that bad. Please. We can fix this. Please do not do this."

In response, Richard turned his back on his pleading wife. He opened the door, placed his apartment keys in the bowl on the table stand above the shoe rack and said, "This is goodbye, Marge."

Marge could only watch as her husband walked out into the hallway. When he turned the hallway corner that chilly feeling in

Marge's breast exploded. It was as if she had taken a deep breath of liquid nitrogen. Her chest was a frozen tundra. Siberia could not be colder. It took all of Marge's immediate concentration to continue breathing.

At this moment, if anyone entered the apartment hallway, they would see door twelve ajar. They would see Marge Reeves, in a pink robe, on her knees and rear with her arms hugging her chest. And they would see a river of warm tears streaming down her cheeks. Sometime later, Marge felt small arms wrap around her neck and shoulders. The coldness in her breast was pushed away instantaneously and the tears magically shut off. Marge was brought back to reality by Sophia's touch.

"Everything is going to be okay mom," said Sophia. Her young head was buried in her mother's sweet-smelling hair.

Marge reached up and softly disengaged her daughters grasp. She wiped her tears on the sleeve of the robe and stood up. Then Marge closed the apartment door, locked it, and turned to face her saving grace.

As Sophia saw her mom's face she said, "You need a tissue."

"And you said you needed a glass of water," replied Marge with a forced smile.

Together the Reeves ladies entered the kitchen and got what they needed. Afterwards they went back to bed and cuddled.

Act IV: H E L L

DUNE
HOT

Google "The Old Man's Hymn." - A

Wispy and feathery cirrus clouds streaked across the bright blue sky. On this day, the sun shined with a summer might that made the day particularly hot.

Liam Cavallone had just entered the shotgun seat of Bruce's black Dodge Caravan and offered him props. He then placed his soccer gear on the floor by his feet. Before Liam could say hi to the rest of the guys, Bruce said, "I got the perfect playlist for this ride."

"I've have never *ever* doubted you," returned Liam.

"Cap, that's cap," said Raza from the back of the van.

Liam smiled and Jamie said, "Yo, I need a coffee before this game. Can we stop at a Tims?"

"No can-do bossman," answered Bruce. He turned the key and ignited the van. "Armstrong said the game is at one and we're *already* late."

"Plus, it's too hot for coffee," said Liam. "Drink some water; what's on the playlist?"

"Ugh," sounded Jamie.

Bruce turned on the music and "All Falls Down" by Kanye West began to play.

"All *Ye*," Bruce said.

"Ill," said Raza.

Air conditioning accompanied by Kanye West play in the

background as Bruce drove to the location of the scrimmage match. The tinted windows add to the coolness. Raza and Jamie enjoyed this moment on their cell phones.

"What you guys playin' now?" questioned Liam.

Raza and Jaime started giggling.

Jamie whispered to Raza, "Hehehe – he doesn't know. Hehehe s-should we tell him?"

"We are in the same van; I can hear you!" said the annoyed captain.

"Bro chillout, It's Pokémon Go," said Raza. "Lmao he sounds pissed."

"*Bro, chill out*," mimicked Liam.

Raza laughed and Bruce said, "Yo, Jamie tell Liam what you told me. About the girl from the other high school."

"Ye," said Jamie. "Dig it. We were playin' Pokémon Go down at Bayfront, like a week ago, and I started mackin' on this chick."

"You can't say *mackin' on this chick,*" complained Raza. "Like what did you actually say to her?"

"*Bruh!* I simply asked what Pokémon she used and what team she was on," said Jamie.

"And then what happened after?" prodded Bruce. He had made his way down the mountain using the Jolley Cut.

"We literally started dating after, *like* uh two dates," said Jamie. "And she's literally a dime too, no cap. The only bad thing is that we are on different teams. I'm Mystic, blue, and she's Valor, red. We probably should breakup *cause* she said we're basically Romeo and Juliet."

"For sure bud," said Bruce. "And you're Juliet."

The whole van started to laugh pleasantly; Jamie laughed sarcastically.

"Har har har, you said that last time," said Jamie. "But I swear they be calling us that."

"Jamie, that's legit a cool story," said Liam. "Bruce, does Penelope play Pokémon Go too?"

"I know it's cool," said Jamie to himself.

"Hold the phone," said Bruce. "Why do you want to know that?"

"So, I can rob a bank with her," said Liam sarcastically. "To play Pokémon Go with her! What do *you* think?"

"Bruh, we *don't* date sisters," said Raza. Bruce and Jamie nodded their heads solemnly in agreement. "We can joke about smashing moms and smashing sisters *but* we don't actually smash, or *date*, moms or sisters. That's just how it is."

"Okay, hear me out," began Liam. "What if we both liked each other."

"Ew, that's stupid bro," said Jamie.

Raza quickly and forcefully pushed air out of his nose and suppressed a smile.

Before Liam could protest Bruce said, "It's hella stupid and we're here."

With the press of a button "Everything We Need" by Kanye West is turned off.

"Get out," said Bruce.

"Ugh," said Jaime. "It's going to be ridiculously hot out there."

"Even more reason to stay hydrated," said Liam.

Raza gathered his belongings. The sounds of sports bags being raised filled the cool space. Jamie opened the door of Bruce's van.

"I'm legally blind," he said.

From outside the van door the sun beamed him. He raised his hand to shield his sight from the blinding rays. Next, he leaped out from the dark cool van as a frog might leap out of some bushes into a local pond.

As Jamie's flipflops met the parking lot cement, the scorched outside air swiftly moved into the van. Raza felt the dryness and swallowed. *It's going to be a hot game,* thought Raza.

"Earth to Raza," said Bruce. "We've got a game to win."
"Roger, roger," robotically said Raza from his seat.

...

Ten minutes later, the group of soccer players were situated around their nice bench on the north side of McMaster's prestigious soccer field. While by the bench, Liam noticed several of the other team members on their way to the other side of the field. He recalled coach Armstrong's words, "I've organized a friendly match for us next week. We will be playing the best team in our division. Only the best for my team."

"We haven't played them yet," said Jamie. "Right, Cap'?"

Raza, Bruce, and Jamie were lacing up their cleats.

Already prepared, with his arms across his chest, Liam said, "Not yet. We haven't played the Knights this season."

"We play in two weeks," informed Bruce.

"And they finished first last year?" Offered Raza.

"Ye," answered Jamie grimly.

"Hmmm," said Raza thoughtfully.

"Should make for a fun friendly match," said Bruce. "Here comes the rest of our team."

Jamie and Raza's heads snapped up to witness the rest of their team making their way to the green turf field. The searing sun glared down on upon them all. Most had baseball hats or sunglasses on.

When Raza was prepared to play, he checked his cell phone. At the same time, Bruce and Jamie got up from the bench. Liam took a swig from his water bottle. Raza's eyes saw that they had exactly twenty-one minutes before the start of the game.

"Yo Raza, take these guys out by the net and practice passing the ball back and forth," said Liam. "I'll wait for the rest of the team."

Eager to warm up in the hot sun Jaime said, "What an amazing idea. I can't wait to sweat to death before the game starts." He then stretched. With his fingers he touched his toes.

From the bench, Bruce kicked a soccer ball. The ball soared gracefully though the sky into the mesh. Raza's eyebrows raised. He was impressed. *Bruce must be practicing*, thought Raza.

"Go fetch, Jamie," said Raza.

"Bark, bark," responded Jamie.

Raza watched as Jamie chased towards the ball. He rolled his eyes and put his cell phone back in his duffle bag. He made sure to wrap it in the soft orange towel he kept in his bag. Once his cell phone was cradled in the cloth, he zipped up his bag and placed it under the nice bench. Raza raised from his seat and followed Jamie's path, behind Bruce.

"Maybe we should put on some sunscreen," said Bruce. He was stretching his arms and shaking out his stiff legs.

Raza caught up to Bruce and said, "It should get cloudy soon-ish. That's what the weather app reported."

Raza heard a thud and Bruce saw the ball roll over towards them.

Jamie had gotten the ball out from the net and kicked it towards the two walking over. On the green vibrant turf, the ball moved swiftly.

Bruce's left shoulder pushed into Raza's and Bruce stepped towards the incoming ball. As Bruce's feet collected the ball, with both hands, Raza pulled at Bruce's left wrist.

"Oi!" said Bruce.

Momentarily, Bruce was pulled backwards, and Raza rushed forward. Raza collected the stationary ball and ran towards the net. Bruce shook his head and followed Raza's long strides.

"Try me!" called out Jamie from the goal line. Jamie stood and taunted Raza with the call of his right hand. He did so in the style of Bruce Lee.

At the 18-yard box, Raza struck the ball with the laces of his right foot. The ball moved speedily. The keeper leapt to his right and caught the powerful shot in the center of his chest.

"Solid strike," said Jamie.

"I would have scored," announced Bruce.

The three players were already sweaty.

"Passing!" said Liam. With boldness, his voice carried over the pitch. Raza looked to Liam and back at the bench. He saw his team getting ready. Farther down, on the opposite side of the field, he saw a few of the Knights passing a ball around.

Raza heard his teammates passing the ball back and forth. These sounds remind him of his duty. So, he turns around and jogs over to meet up with them. When he gets closer to Bruce, who currently has the ball at his feet, Raza sprints past and makes a long run.

"Coach Armstrong is here!" announced Liam.

Liam's loud voice distracted Bruce and the ball is kicked with extra power. The long pass sailed over Raza's head.

Raza turned his body and sprints to where he assumed the ball will stop.

"Back to the bench!" called Liam.

In response, above his head, Raza presented a thumbs up. Meanwhile, his long strides chased after the ball. Raza crossed the maroon running track that outlined the field and noticed that his cleats spring up. His eyes followed the ball. It rests in a field of yellow dandelions. As the team huddled around Armstrong, Raza's right foot made contact with the misguided soccer ball.

He stepped four paces away from the ball and looked to where he wanted it to go. Raza then took a deep breath and kicked the ball with all his might.

He watched as the white ball soars far above the cross bar. Its headed towards the bench. Raza witnessed the white circle eclipse the sun. Liam, anticipated Raza's kick, is by the bench prepared to gather the ball.

Sweat drips down Raza's forehead as he stood and watched Liam collect the ball. A gentle breeze reminded Raza that he needed to get back to his team. Before he began to jog back, Raza looked to where he had just struck the ball. He noticed that his kick had left a small divot of exposed earth. Additionally, there is a single dandelion removed from the earth.

SUSPICIOUS
SCOUT

There is common ancestry among us all. - A

"Forget our warmup," Coach Armstrong says. "It's hot enough to make your blood boil."

The Braves senior boys' soccer team sit in the shade of the nice McMaster bench. The stone canopy blocks the sun's relentlessness. Coach Armstrong stands in front of his team with his arms across his mighty chest. He is wearing a black baseball hat that says "Coach" and reflective sunglasses.

"Trevor, my lad, would you kindly pass me my white board. Beside the black notebook. Yes, that one. And a marker. Many thanks. Now, since today is a friendly match, the starting lineup will not change. We got Bruce as sweeper - "

"Captains please!" yells the referee from the center of the field.

Coach Armstrong makes eye contact with Liam. With a sudden movement of his head, he indicates the captain should go meet up with the ref. Wordlessly, Liam understands and jogs towards the center circle.

"Good afternoon, gentlemen," begins the ref.

Liam notices that the ref is an older man and that on his bald head rests a stylish bucket hat. The captain of the Knights is standing directly in front of Liam. His hair is long, black and, is tied up into a knot. *The Knights' black and gold uniform cannot feel good in this heat*, thinks Liam. The sun is in the Knights eyes, so his hands are placed above his eyebrows.

"I run a tight ship. However, we have no linesmen. It's just me. So, if any calls are missed or any offsides go unobserved... all I can say is that I'll do my best to watch for that." The ref's voice is strong and steady. "With that out of the way, its fiendishly hot out here and I was told this is a friendly match. So, let's have a good clean game and since the Braves already paid me cold hard cash, they get to call it in the air."

Magically, the ref manages to wink at both players and flip a coin into the air.

At the toonies third rotation Liam calls, "Tails."

The toonie lands in the ref's open palm. With a swift movement, he then places it on top of the back of his other.

The captain of the Knights could not look more bored. Impatiently, he is tapping his right foot against the green vibrant turf. The referee reveals the coin.

"Tails it is. You want first possession? Or a side to start?" asks the ref.

After a quick moment of thought Liam says, "They can start, and we'll stay on this side."

"Alright," comments the ref. "Lemme see you shake and then we start in three. Good luck gentlemen; let's have a good clean match."

Liam shakes hands with the captain of the Knights. He is perturbed by the Knights' sweaty grip. After that it's game on.

...

Within three minutes of play time, Raza scores against the Knights. The black and gold fail their first attack and Bruce, the Braves' sweeper, collects the ball by the Braves' eighteen-yard box. While the Knight defenders are caught sleeping, Raza makes a mad dash. Bruce, with no current pressure, sees Raza's rapid movement and is aware of where he should send the ball next.

Bruce kicks the ball. It goes high above everyone. Some of the Knight defenders stand still and watch as the ball soars above. Raza, already in motion, meets the ball behind the last line of defenders.

A futile yell from the Knights keeper can be heard by all. His anger at his defender's lack of awareness is palpable. Regardless, the keeper prepares to save the strike.

Raza, on a clear breakaway, runs with the ball towards the Knights goalie. He is surprised when the keeper doesn't come out to challenge him. So, calmly, with his eyes, Raza picks out the left goal post and, at the top of the box, strikes the ball with all his force.

The ref's whistle marks the first goal of the match. Cheers from the Braves bench can be heard, as well as, from the McMaster bleachers. Unseen until now, Raza grasps that there is a small crowd of observers on the grand stone bleachers. He wasn't expecting anyone spectators today. *This is just a friendly,* thinks Raza.

A couple of his teammates surround him, pat him on the back and congratulate him on the goal. With his teammates Raza jogs to the center circle in preparation for the next kick-off. On the way back, he assumes the crowd is made up of parents and siblings.

...

After nine minutes of playtime Jamie, the Braves right-wing defender, runs shoulder to shoulder with the Knights attacker. As the stalwart Knight entered the Braves eighteen-yard box he is suddenly overthrown by the shoulder of Jamie. Jamie is at a loss at this sudden moment of weakness. Instantly the referee blows his whistle for a penalty shot.

Coach Armstrong stands tall with vigilant stoicism. A chorus of criticism can be heard from his bench which are matched by the chorus of cheers from the Knights bench.

Back on the field, Liam lines up on the top of the box beside Raza. The two Braves are catching their breath. They, as well as several others, prepare to chase after the ball in the chance that there is a rebound. After the referee finishes his talk with the Braves keeper and the captain of the Knights, the penalty shot is moments away.

The referee places the ball at the designated spot. Then, he backs away to watch the kick. At the sound of the whistle, the captain of the Knights steps three paces back. The Braves keeper stands on the goal line and attempts to look as big as humanly possible.

Raza feels a soft breeze on the back of his neck and then hears the ref's final whistle. The captain of the Knights runs up and kicks the ball with enormous power. The keeper attempts to predict the shot and jumps towards his right goal post. The ball is struck dead straight; it goes into to back of the net.

A whistle breaks the solemn silence. Roars of approval follow swiftly behind.

Liam walks over to his keeper and says, "Ay no sweat; nice try."

He offers a hand to the Brave. The goalie's glove accepts, and he is raised to his feet.

"Yeah, I thought for sure he was going to kick it here," returns the crestfallen keeper.

As the teams reset for kickoff, the coach of the Knights asks the referee if the players may take a water break. The ref looks towards Armstrong for agreement. In response Armstrong offers a thumbs up.

At the center of the field another whistle is heard.

"Ten-minute water break!" yells the ref.

The opposing teams return to their bench. Water bottles are retrieved. Thirsts are quenched. The respite is well deserved.

Raza observes that soft white clouds are coming towards the field. They remind him of Toy Story. Breath on the Braves bench is caught, and a momentary peace is established.

"You guys see that guy in the back?" asks Bruce.

"That guy with the white hat on?" questions Jamie.

"Don't take notice of him," comments coach Armstrong. "He's a *scoundrel.*"

The team perks up to keenly listen.

"He's an old teammate of mine and he's a scout," finishes the coach.

"So, you're telling us," begins Liam, "that man," he points, with his right index finger, "is a head-hunter?"

"That's what I'm telling you," confirms coach Armstrong. "And, that it is rude to point."

Liam immediately lowers his hand and after a brief silence coach Armstrong says, "However, the coach of the Knights was also a teammate of ours. So, the other team should know this as well."

Raza smiles knowingly. Not because he knew the connection between the coaches. But because he sees this as an opportunity to shine.

A north wind blows through the field. It's a firm gust of air that pulls jerseys against skin and cools sweat.

Moments later the whistle is blown. Ten minuities have passed, and the water break concludes.

The game continues from the last action. The Braves start with the ball at center. The referee blows the whistle, and the striker kicks the ball back to Liam, to the center of midfield.

He turns to his left and kicks the ball wide. The Braves left-wing player collects the ball and notices incoming pressure. In response, he puts his body in-between the incoming attacker and the ball. The Knights striker attempts to steal the ball but is unable. The Brave decides to pass the ball backwards to his open defender.

Jamie has anticipated the pass and has already decided where the ball should go next. First time, the defender strikes the ball up and over the players towards the center of the field. There, Raza collects the ball with ease. Suddenly, three Knights players move towards Raza. He is surrounded.

Witnessing this, Liam makes a snap decision. He runs down the right wing and yells, "Raza! Here!"

Raza pushes the ball through the legs of one Knights player and without looking kicks the ball towards the voice of his captain.

During this time Liam has already outrun the defenders and collects the free ball with no pressure.

He then cuts towards the Knights net. Knights players are panting in the attempt to catch up. He glances up from the ball and notices the Knights keeper running towards him. The goalie has just past the eighteen-yard box and is already seven yards away from Liam.

Another snap decision is made. With opposition chasing behind and the keeper directly in front, Liam chips the ball high. It sails right over the advancing goalie. The chasing Knights stop dead in their tracks and watch.

From the Braves bench someone says, "It's going over the net."

"Nah man, he literally hit it perfect," responds another.
Parallel to when the penalty shot was taken, breaths are held. The keeper of the Knights turns around and curses like a sailor. He watches helplessly as the ball bounces on the six-yard box and nonchalantly rolls across the goal line. The referee's whistle pierces the silence.

Fervent applause can be heard from the grand stone bleachers, and from the Braves bench. Even the Knights bench shows acknowledgment for the cheeky goal. Although it is a minimal display.
As the teams walk back to their respective sides, a Knights player attacks Jamie verbally. It is a weak, mindless, throwaway comment that sends him into a rage.

"You, absolute toxic ASS!" yells Jamie.

The aggression attracts attention from both teams. With the ears of an elephant, the referee notices and blows his whistle. He then says, "Halftime. Go cool off."

...

At half time the friendly game is two to one, in favor of the Braves.

"I'm not going to say anything," states coach Armstrong.

The Braves sit at their nice bench breathing heavily and sweating. Raza hears quick shallow breaths and deep gulps of water. He, himself is sweating profusely. In response to his body Raza opens his bag and retrieves his towel. The cell phone gently rolls out of the soft orange towel and falls into the darkness of the bag. He then uses the towel to wipe the sweat off his forehead and back.

After five long minutes coach Armstrong says, "We're going to make some minor changes at the beginning of the second half. Other than that, you guys know what to do and *how* to do it. Remember, although this is a *friendly,* knowing how to execute is vital."

…

Raza watches the second half kick off from the bench.

"You're going in soon, Raza," says Armstrong. "You're sitting off to refresh your legs. Good early goal."

"Yes, coach," says Raza, "and thanks, coach."
Before Raza goes back on the pitch, he notices three key points. The first is that several players on the Knights bench are not-so subtly pointing at the scout. The second is that, on the field, the Knights are playing with obvious aggression. Their tackles have become increasingly physical. Raza believes it's only a matter of time before the referee has to call something. Which leads to the third point. Raza has already witnessed the ref miss two calls. *He is clearly oblivious*, thinks Raza.

A Knight player grabs the bottom of a Braves jersey and yanks. The Brave is thrown off balance and clumsily hits the ball out of play. The whistle is blown, and a Knight prepares to throw the ball back in.

With his chest, Liam intercepts the Knights throw in and brings the ball to his feet. From behind, a Knight player slide tackles and takes him out.

The ball rolls to another Brave and the play continues.

"No call again?" says coach Armstrong. His shoulders are raised and palms open. He has a frustrated look on his face.

With an abruptness the whistle is blown.

"Second-half water break!" announces the referee.

Grumbles and frustrated sounds are heard from the Braves and the Knights. While clouds have shaded the playing field and the air has cooled down considerably the players leave the field unhappy. The Knights wished they had at least tied during the opening of the second half. And the Braves dislike the missed calls.

The next five minutes are spent drinking water and catching breath. Minor changes are made by both teams. Eager to close out the game, the players retake the field.

...

After two minutes of play Liam has possession of the ball. He is at the center of the field, on the left side. The ball is dangerously close to the out of bounds line. In fact, Liam has the ball on the white line and at his back is an aggressive Knight. With a hasty swiftness another Knight comes and, with malice, steps on Liam's left foot.

The whistle is blown instantly.

"Holy Fuck! That's a yellow!" yells the Brave keeper from his net. His voice carries over all the other noise. "He blatantly stomped on him! I could see it from here!"

"One more word and I'll give *you* a yellow!" responds the referee. The Braves keep is forced into silence.

"Number seven; right here. This is your *only* warning. Anything else and you're *done*."

Raza attends to Liam. There is a small circle of players around the downed player. Some Knights and Braves have taken a knee as they wait for what's to come. Raza notices the captain's face is a mask of suffering.

"We need assistance now," comments Raza to no one in particular.

Coach Armstrong is right behind and says, "Assistance is here. Back up gentlemen; let him breath. Can you move your feet son?"

Liam nods his head slowly. As he attempts to move his left foot, he lets out a painful howl.

"Okay this is no good," comments the coach. "Raza, go run to the stands and get Liam's father. He needs to be taken to the hospital."

Raza nods once and is off to complete the task.

"Okay, here's what is going to happen Liam," continues Armstrong. "Breath deep and focus on your breath. In a moment, together, we are going to stand. And then, with me at your side, we will limp over to the bench. Do not put any pressure on your left foot. There your father will come to collect you and then take you to the hospital. Do you understand?"

"Yes sir," says Liam. He stabilizes his breath and prepares for further pain.

...

Five minutes later play is resumed. Ten minutes later Liam is in his father's car and beginning his journey to the hospital. Fifteen minutes later, right before the end of play, Raza scores the last goal of the game.

...

Raza doesn't get hot with rage. He goes cold. The thought of shining for the scout is completely removed. An icy determination has replaced it. While Raza cools into a blizzard storm, the referee announces that there will be no additional time due to the heat and the fact that this is a friendly match.

With minutes left in playtime the Knights team captain strikes from distance and misses. The Braves have possession of the ball, and the keeper prepares to take a goal kick.

Even before the ref's whistle, Raza is in motion. He began his run at the edge of the field. And with speed, his long strides bring him to the opposite side of the pitch.

The Braves keeper spots the speedy maroon jersey as it passes behind and in front of black and gold jerseys. A wicked smart kick places the ball a third way down the Knights side of the field.

Raza jumps to meet the ball. In the air, a Knights defender challenges him. Another awaits the outcome.

The ace of the Braves meets the descending ball first. He hits the ball off his head, high up and forward. The ball is hit over the head of both his challengers and Raza runs to collect the ball once more. It bounces lively off the green vibrant turf towards the Knights' net. The two defenders grunt and chase after Raza.

While in a full sprint, Raza notices the Knights keeper is at his eighteenyard box and is on his way to meet the ball. Both players are about an equal distance away. Gritting his teeth, Raza pushes himself. With a burst of speed, he beats the Knights keeper to the ball by three strides. Raza then performs a Ronaldo chop. With his right foot, he quickly chops the ball to his left side. The last Knight is beaten at the top of his box.

Under minimal pressure Raza slows down. Some Knights players are chasing him. Others have given up and have accepted the inevitable outcome. Braves, on the bench and on the field, are already celebrating.

While still in possession of the ball, Raza saunters forward towards the empty net. The ball crosses the six-yard box. It rolls to the goal line. Raza's foot stops the ball there. He looks back to his net. He savours this moment for a fraction of a second and then taps the ball over the goal line.

The ref blows the whistle, announcing the goal and the end of the match.

KING
HOSPITAL

A million deaths have been counted at this hospital. - A

Exactly forty-two minutes after Liam Cavallone was struck down, he and his father had arrived at the hospital.

His white RDX Acura pushed over the speed bump and under the automated arm. Without increasing speed, he patrolled the front parking lot, and searched for an open spot. Unable to find an available spot in the front, Carmine was forced to navigate his car to the back of the hospital. Serendipitously, he found parking under an old tree and noticed that he has already passed by the entrance to emergency care.

Once Carmine had parked, he checked the digital car clock. It read 5:15 p.m. He felt anxious for his injured son and for Arianna's impromptu soup kitchen. Both hurdles occurred so suddenly.

Quickly, Carmine recalled how both events began. Several days ago, with the mediator, he and Arianna both agreed to organize a charitable event. A giving back to the local community in the form of a soup kitchen. Additionally, Arianna intended this event to be her last hurrah at the Cavallone restaurant. She would depart from the restaurant immediately after to pursue an entirely different career. However, this was their first time. The restaurant did not truly know how this impromptu event would go. He dreaded to inform her about their son's injury. He would text her the details, but only *after* the doctor had seen him.

As the father, Carmine felt his son's injury as it was his own. As he watched from the grand stone bleachers the injury had looked horrid. When his son took the first slide tackle Carmine's cool head was disturbed, but when Liam's foot was blatantly stepped on, he totally lost his cool. The malice displayed by the other player and the awkwardness of Liam's fall sent shivers down Carmine's spine.

To combat these anxious thoughts Carmine practiced a breathing meditation he picked up from the divorce mediator. With slow controlled breaths he established a calm demeanor. Carmine reminded himself that he was grateful for the quick commute. There had been minimal traffic and the sun was obscured by fluffy clouds. The clouds made him feel optimistic. Present situation excluded; the day would turn out lovely. Carmine achieved this enforced peace within several breaths.

...

Inside St. Joe's hospital, at the emergency care front reception desk, sat Sabetha Belmont. The older British lady sat with a relaxed posture that came from the three years she had been working there. On the desk, beside the personal computer, was a beat-up copy of her late husband's favourite story, *The Strange Case of Dr. Jekyll and Mr. Hyde*. Sabetha was lost in thought.

When Sabetha was bored, she reviewed the hospital departments in her head. On the first floor there was the surgery center and eye clinic. Which drew the most appointments. Additionally, on the first floor, there was a foot clinic and an office for mental health. Below, on the ground floor, was the large Dialysis unit, a minor plastic surgery center and a stay well program, for the elderly. Sabetha was in the accepted age range for the stay well program. However, her pride and decent physical health kept her away from such activities.

At 5:31 p.m. Sabetha witnessed a tall boy, dressed in a soccer uniform, limp past the emergency care doors. The sliding automated doors moved with quiet efficiency and the boy had to lean against an equally tall man in order to move. Sabetha presumed this was the father. A nurse passing by also witnessed the slow awkward trip and offered the suffering boy a wheelchair. The father graciously accepted the kind offer.

The nurse returned with a wheel chair and haste. In a quick moment Liam was seated in a reliable leather wheelchair. From behind the glass wall, Sabetha saw the instant relief brought to the boys' face. The father thanked the nurse and the nurse returned to his duties.

Sabetha met the stare of the father, and she used her right hand to wave him over.

"Good evening, gentlemen," said Sabetha. Her voice came out strong but was slightly muffled by the fiber glass. The glass was there to sustain a safe distance from the patients.

"Hello there," returned Carmine.

"Bellow bear?" questioned Sabetha.

Carmine coughed and repeated, "Hello there."

From behind the glass Sabetha readjusted her thick glasses. At the same time, she also adjusted her hearing aids. The device had been turned off for the past four minutes.

"Yes, yes," the receptionist said. "The boy's health card here, please."

Sabetha's right ringed index finger pointed to the square opening at the bottom of the glass.

From the wheelchair, Liam noticed a black pearl ring on the old lady's index finger. He thought it looked badass.

Carmine had anticipated the need for the health card. He had already retrieved his son's card from the car. He removed the card from his brown leather wallet and placed it, facing towards Sabetha, at the space between the glass.

In an instant, the receptionist was activated. Liam could hear quick clicks and rapid typing. He next heard the receptionist ask, "Address?"

"21 Marmalade drive," answered Carmine.

"21 Harama-blade drive?" asked Sabetha.

"21 Marmalade drive," repeated Carmine.

"Oh, with a 'N'," said Sabetha with indifference. "21 Narnia drive."

"With a 'M'," said Liam. "Marm-ma-lade."

"I've got it," said Sabetha. The clicking and typing continued throughout the conversation. "Work related?" she asked.

"Well, it occurred at a high school soccer game," Carmine began. "Another player-"

Sabetha raised her right hand to stop the gentleman. She then said, "Not work related."

Click.

"Sorry but save it," she said flatly. As she spoke a small dark device beside her computer started to hum.

"The nurse will hear the W's. Why, when, where, what, and who. Here. Put this on your son's wrist." The small dark device printed out a slip of paper. She passed him the plastic wristband with small print on it.

Carmine noticed it had his son's name on it.

"Keep it on while he's in the hospital."

Presently, Sabetha pointed her bony finger to the open waiting room on the left. "You can wait there until the triage nurse calls you," she said.

"Thank you," said Liam.

"And have a nice evening," said Carmine.

In response Sabetha nodded her head just once and reopened her beat-up novel.

...

Carmine and Liam sat in the empty waiting room.

"Hey," said Carmine.

"Yeah?" said Liam. His eyebrows raise but his eyes remain closed.

"Remember when you tripped rollerblading?"

"Yeah, how could I forget? I couldn't get my hands out fast enough and I fell on my lips." Liam's right hand touched his lips in remembrance.

"Yeah, they were cut up pretty bad."

"We didn't go to urgent care for that."

"Nope," said Carmine. "You were spitting blood. Swallowed a tooth and yet that busted lip healed quick."

In the comfortable silence that followed some of Liam's fears were quelled.

"Lorenzo, is different story," said Carmine.

Before either could speak any further, the overhead speaker system called Liam's number. They were told to proceed to window three.

"Liam and Carmine, I presume," said the nurse.

Behind the protected desk, a male nurse is seated in a casual position behind a computer screen. The nurse has caramel coloured skin and his voice comes out suave.

"Present," answered Liam.

Beside Liam's wheelchair there is a simple chair and Carmine sits down.

"My name is Raoul," the nurse replied. "Before we get into it, for your file and the report, I am required to ask you some questions." Raoul took their silence as understanding. "Are you currently on any medication?"

Liam looked to his father before he said, "No medication currently."

"Well put," replied Raoul. "The last time you were injured was, uh, when? Do you remember?"

With his right hand, Liam scratched the top of his head. "Uhh I'm not sure when," began Liam. "But I remember it was because of a nasty bee sting."

Carmine said, "That was six years ago. Around the summertime. I remember because I swatted the bee on your back. The swelling from the sting wouldn't go down."

"Nice," confirmed Raoul. "Well not nice, but that matches what we have on file." Raoul makes eye contact with Liam and said, "So what happened today?"

"My left foot got stomped on," answered Liam. His shoulders raise, as if to say I couldn't help it. "And now there's a constant pain. It's manageable."

"On of scale of ten, where ten is the most pain you've ever experienced in your life and one is a bunny headbutting your, um leg, rate your current pain."

"Uh, about a two."

"And before?"

"A solid nine or eight."

"Solid nine," repeated Raoul and he typed that on Liam's file. As Raoul continued to type on his computer, Carmine and Liam wait in polite silence.

"Well, gentlemen," said Raoul, "I got some good news and some bad news. The bad news is that you're going to need an x-ray. It's a painless procedure but just by looking at the area of trauma, well, it doesn't look good. Your foot shows clear evidence of internal bludgeoning. That being said, the good news is that you won't have to wait long. At the moment, there are no other patients in urgent care. So, as soon as your xray is completed the doctor will see you right away. If I had to estimate, you'll be all good to go in fifteen to twenty minutes."

The Cavallone men nod their heads.

Raoul continued, "Just down that corridor over there is our x-ray unit, you can't miss it. If you do, you'll hit the cafeteria. Once there, our technician will take care of you. And then you'll have to come back this way to see the doctor. Any questions?"

"Nope," replied Liam.

"That was perfect," replied Carmine.
"Wonderful, well, you're all good to go," concluded Raoul.

...

Eleven minutes after, Liam and Carmine wait in an urgent care area. It smells sterilized with hints of lemon and is closed off by beige curtains. Liam sits atop the standard grey patient's bed and Carmine stands dutifully beside. They wait for the doctor.

There is a cough at the curtain door.

"I'm coming in," said the doctor. "I am Doctor Baz. Greetings. You appear stable, but how do you feel?"

Carmine and Liam are greeted by a stout Indian gentleman. Immediately, Carmine's sensitive nose smelled herbs and spices. Dr. Baz just finished his lunch which he had to cut short.

"I feel uh adequate," announced Liam. "I know my foot is injured but overall, I'm okay."

"Adequate!" responded Dr. Baz. He fully opens the curtains and reveals the back of urgent care. "Good word, adequate. Lost in scrabble to my mother-in-law because of that word. There are no other patients in so let's open it up, shall we?"

By opening the bed curtains the doctor revealed several other open and prepared beds. The nurse's station is exposed thus showing copier machines, digital screens, supplies and mountains of paperwork.

"You must be Liam's father, Carmine. Nice to meet you both. Soccer injures are nasty. Ah, that reminds me of a joke my nephew told me. How did it go again? Oh yes! What do you call a tiny soccer player with an orange slice and sticky fingers?"

After a quick moment Carmine asked, "What do you call it doc?"

With a genuine grin Dr. Baz said, "A little messy." Liam responded to the joke by covering his face with his hands and Carmine lets out a defeated laugh.

"Well, it is a dad joke. I'm glad the target audience enjoyed it," said Dr. Baz. He then clears his throat and brings upon a business demeanour. "To put it simply, you broke your pinky toe. Do you see this here? On the print-out of your x-ray. Right here, there is a clear break. Truly unfortunate. Thankfully, it is a clean break and therefore it will heal wonderfully. Next is rehabilitation. Your foot will need to be in a cast. For two weeks at a minimum and a full month at maximum. I can see you're a strong young man so it is highly probable that it will heal quick. However, you should avoid all physical activity. Do you understand? You nod your head. Good. Further physical activity will only antagonize the injury and ensure the healing process will take longer. That's about everything. If there are no questions a nurse will be joining you in a moment to apply your cast. Additionally, if required, we have crutches available. Have a good day and stay off it for a week and you'll be right as rain."

...

At 6:53 p.m. Carmine's white RDX Acura parked at the front of the family restaurant. On the ride back, he informed his son that he had a personal matter he must attend to. So, his mother will take care of him as soon as they arrived the restaurant.

Arianna observed her husband and son as they pulled in front. She is outside the restaurant's main doors, in the now cool weather. Her hair is tied up into a graceful bun and she is wearing a cream-coloured summer dress.

As Carmine dropped off Liam, he told him that he loves him and that he will check on him tomorrow. Arianna is aware of where Carmine is off to. An errand, so the soup kitchen can run smoothly tomorrow. The divorced couple exchange no words and without much difficulty, Arianna helped Liam out of the car and into the restaurant.

"I got you," she said.

Speedily Arianna and Liam move to the kitchen. She has prepared chicken noodle soup with garlic bread. If he was hungry from the soccer game, Liam is now voracious after the hospital. The smell made Liam's mouth salivate. He saw that there are several pots on the oven and a plethora of sandwiches premade. He sits down at the kitchen table and Arianna placed some food in front of him.

Arianna is relieved to see her son eat with such ferocity. Her shoulders relax a little. After he had devoured his meal Arianna asked him if he wanted seconds. In response, Liam nodded his head.

As she finished pouring another bowl of soup, Ariana asked, "Liam, have you seen five hundred dollars anywhere? That amount is gone from the old register."

Liam heard that his mom's voice is calm and non-accusatory. When she placed the second bowl of soup in front of him, Liam said, "Honestly, I have no clue."

"Hmmm," sounded Arianna thoughtfully. She crossed her arms across her chest. "What do you think of Lo'? Does he seem distant to you?"

Liam shrugged and said, "Well yeah, you remember his reaction to the divorce conversation. That was a week ago; he's probably still processing that."

"Well, just now I told him I was going to leave the restaurant."

Liam swallowed some soup and said, "How did he take it?"

"He left and I'm not sure where he went."

Act V: M I G H T Y

FU TURE
PL ANS

O you who know what we suffer here, do not
forget us in your prayers. - A

At 6 p.m. Raza Singh just finished his shower.

Raza chose to wear a pink hoodie with black soccer shorts.
The air conditioning in the Singh house made it feel chilly.
Furthermore, Raza's sensitivity to the cold is known.

He exited the second-floor washroom. However, Before Raza
left, he ensured that he the room is as it was before him. So, with
his towel, Raza wiped the pristine countertop. With his foot he
positioned the snug white rug back in its centered spot and he
even wiped the front facing mirror, which is framed in opulent
jewels. Thus, the immaculate washroom is restored to the way it
was before.

Raza hummed to himself as he made his way downstairs. On his
way down, his right-hand trailed along the glossy banister and
he hopped down the magnificent steps. He was in an effervescent
mood.

"So that's' what Dr. Burrows has been up to," Raza heard his
father say.

Raza heard his father even before he saw him. For the door
behind the open style living area was left ajar. As Raza entered
the inviting living room, he can now see his mother and father
outside.

It looks utterly divine where his parents are seated. In the
Singh backyard, under the luxurious light green canopy, sit a
comfortable Kunal and Jiya Singh. While under the cover of
shade, the weather is perfect. Warmly cool. Atop the fantastic
mesh table are three cups of honey riced green tea as well as an
invasive dialogue.

"Indeed, and did you hear that a rather new professor was caught sleeping with a student?" questioned Jiya. Raza was astounded hearing his mothers, usually timid voice, come out with strength.

Raza's parents are still dressed in what they wore to his soccer match. For Jiya that meant a fancy white summer hat and a tight, yet modest light blue dress. On the table, beside her tea was her expensive sun glasses. Her lavish slippers were left by the backyard door. For Kunal, that meant a deep brown dress shirt and some slacks. Paired with some sharp dress shoes.

"Deplorable," responded a disappointed Kunal. "But which new professor got caught?" He asked. His voice was filled with a misguided sense of hope. "We keep bets in our department."

Unfaltering Raza continued on his path towards his parents. This is not the first time he has heard his parents' gossip. In fact, on the way over he thought of the perfect quip to add. However, before he could speak, there was a proud knock at the front door. This alerted all the Singh's attention.

With casualness Kunal meets his son's eyes. He noticed that Raza is at the threshold of the door.

"My dear Raza, can you attend to that for us," said Jiya. "We are hopelessly relaxed and can't afford to be bothered."

Raza offered his parents finger guns and then said, "I'm on it."

"Hmm, I wonder who it could be," said Jiya Singh.

"My sweet," said Kunal, "we are of the same mind."

...

The proud knock is heard once more. Like his parents, Raza ponders at who could be at the door. He arrived at the pristine front door at exactly 6:13 p.m. Through the distorted stain glass, on the front door, Raza distinguished that the unknown guest is a tall man. With his right hand, Raza opened the pristine front door.

Outside the Singh's front door was the gentleman with a white hat. Raza's thoughts take a shot of expresso.
That's the scout. That's Armstrong's past teammate. He was at the game. I scored two goals. That's a nice hat. That's the scout, Raza thought.

"Raza Singh," said the gentleman in the white Panama hat. His voice came out like his knock. Solid and proud.

Raza observed that the gentleman was also wearing black sunglasses, a pristine white dress shirt and clean beige slacks. At his side, in his left hand, there was a manila folder and on his feet are some scuffed white tennis shoes.

"I am he," stated Raza.

...

"Honey!" said Jiya. "I too thought he played marvelous."

"Straightforward, *determined*, intelligent," listed Kunal.

Jiya took a sip of her tea. The tea tasted delectable.

"Like a viper he is. And he adapts, he scores, he wins. I'm not sure where he got this superb athletic trait. He did not get it from me, nor you, for that matter."

Jiya noticed that Raza was on his way back from dealing with the unknown guest. With her hand she tapped the mesh table.

"He's coming back," announced Jiya in a whisper.

Kunal promptly changed the topic of conversation.

"You know, my sweet, some of the grad students are quite remarkable."

Jiya said, "In what way, my love?"

By now Raza heard his mother and father. He caught his mom saying, "my love," and instinctively repressed his disgust by rolling his eyes. In his hands was the manila folder.

"There is this single father working towards his masters," said Kunal.

Jiya's eyebrows raised. She is genuinely curious.

"He's sharper than a whip," Kunal continued, "he always has the perfect quip. He's a true scholar; a real thirst for knowledge. And unfortunately, he's spread quite thin."

Raza joined his parents at the mesh table. Without interrupting his father, Raza placed the manila folder down and took a sip of his lukewarm honey riced green tea. Raza savoured the delicious taste. It tasted even better in his good mood.

"Spread thin how?" inquired Raza.

"Hmm the soccer star is interested, is he?" questioned Kunal.

"Do continue, my love," said Jiya.

"For you, my sweet, anything. Well, he is a single father. So, taking care of a young daughter is a mountain of a task. Especially during this volatile time. You know, with new technology, the inflation, the pandemic, the war etc. *Take your pick*. I sympathize for parents during this time. I truly do. Additionally, getting your masters is no easy feat. You remember how arduous it was my love. Those long nights writing and researching. Honestly, I occasionally miss it. Ha!" Kunal breathed deep and became a bit somber. "Yesterday he confided in me some truly abysmal information. At the peak of this mountain is a fearsome eagle."

Kunal waited for an inquiring silence to enter the luxurious light green canopy. The polite chirping of birds could be heard during this time of quiet.

"This eagle is the mother of the daughter. She is zealous, vengeful, and utterly tenacious. Like Prometheus, every month, this father awaits patiently for this eagle to consume his liver. It's quite a complicated and deplorable situation. Due to the time, I was unable to dig further, but from what I understood, this mother, without taking care of the child, receives a monthly payout from the single father."

Jiya sat aghast. And Raza is astounded. He can't comprehend the heavy task of parenthood, or single parenthood, but he appreciated his father's eloquent language.

"So," continued Kunal, "While this man takes care of his daughter, solo, he is additionally pursuing a master's degree. *All the while,* he is also attempting to free himself from the legal chains that bind him to this monthly devouring."

"Spread thin. Like butter scraped over too much bread," said Raza.

Jiya's left eyebrow raised appraisingly. "You've been reading Tolkien?" asked Jiya.

"Not yet," answered Raza. "I'm finishing up Dune."

"Ahh Frank Herbert!" said Kunal. "Now there is someone I'd love to have dinner with."

Kunal gave his wife a deliberate glance.

"Yes, yes my love," Jiya said. "I will not organize anymore dinners with the Santana couple. I too have unpleasant memories of that event."

"We are *already* having a dinner conversation. Why did they feel the need to ask that question?" Kunal asked rhetorically.

"Who would you have dinner with? Dead or alive?" asked Raza.

"Yes, that one," responded Jiya. "Let's not get into it. There is a myriad of reasons why we will not have dinner with them again. However, your father focuses on the straw that breaks the camel's back."

"Hmm," sounded Raza.

Kunal cleared his throat and said, "But behold, our son has brought a package!"

"Indeed, gracious father!" responded Raza. He lifted the manila folder in the air as Rafiki did to Simba. "A bright package that is filled with hope."

Jiya scoffed lightly and Kunal is intrigued. Kunal showed a toothy grin.

"Open it, my dear," said Jiya.

"Aye, aye," responded Raza.

Presently, a gentle zephyr blew through the Singh's divine backyard. A sweet fragrant of fresh flowers entered the canopy. At the same time Raza ripped open the manila folder.

Inside are several items. Raza handed them out to his parents. To his father he gave a laminated pamphlet. He then gave his mother a brochure.

"Hmm, what's all this Raza?" questioned Jiya. Her voice was characteristically timid.

"Dear, Mr. Singh," said Raza. His parents turn their attention towards their son. "Congratulations! We are pleased to welcome you to UCLA, and to inform you of your admission for the Fall Quarter," Raza said. His voice is calm and controlled but inside Raza's chest his heart was thumping heavily.

Before he continued, Kunal and Jiya share a look. They also share a foreboding feeling.

"You have already demonstrated your athletic ability and potential for academic success at the University," said Raza. "Umm, UCLA is an exciting and dynamic school. I'm jumping ahead here, as a UCLA student, you will have superior resources available, yes uh, enclosed is a pamphlet of the University and a brochure of, yes yes. Oh here, this is the end bit." Raza cleared his throat, "If you are not already familiar with the picturesque UCLA campus, we encourage you to visit the campus at your convenience. Congratulations again on your achievement. We look forward to your enrollment at the University. Sincerely Devin Lee Anys. That must be the scout's name or the dean. I forgot to ask his name."

Under the luxurious light green canopy, a heavy silence is established. The letter affected each Singh intimately. Raza felt lighter than air. He felt similar to when he received that yellow card for fake proposing. Kunal and Jiya are filled with a deep sense of melancholy. Jiya is saddened at her sudden realization, that her only son is tempted by the idea of moving away from home. Kunal doesn't look forward to what he has to say and in order to remove the bad taste in his mouth he took a generous sip of the honey riced green tea.

"Raza, you will not accept this," simply stated Kunal.

"Wh-,"

Jiya's right hand shot up and demanded silence. Jiya can see that her son's face is utterly confused.

"Let your father explain himself," reasoned Jiya, "this is an open discussion. After you may respond."

Raza was thankful for his mother's wisdom. He feels enraged confusion. He was so surprised at his father's declaration that his thoughts could not formulate.

"I am sorry my son," said Kunal, "this option will not do. Not at all. Your mother and I have established a name at McMaster. *For you.* Your mother and I have spent the last three years at this University. We know where everything is. We have established connections at McMaster. If this is an argument about soccer, what do you have to be worried about? This only confirms you play at a university level. McMaster has a stellar squad. Your superb talent alone grants you a spot on the team. With the connections your mother and I have established it's a guaranteed thing."

During his father's speech Raza was put off but also beguiled. *Clearly my dad has thought this through*, Raza thought.

"Please see that this reckless, unnecessary American trip is above you, my son," finished Kunal.

"Well put, my love," said Jiya. "Before you respond, Raza know that I am on your father's side. We share the same thoughts on this matter."

"I-I-I, hmmm," said Raza. He puts up his hands and makes a T. "Timeout."

Raza crossed his arms across his chest and takes some time to collect his thoughts. *This is a golden ticket*, thought Raza. *Isn't it?*

He still felt disbelief. He also felt anger. *Isn't this offer for me to decide? Do I even want to go to America? That does sound fun.* Raza's thoughts and feelings are like the sea and sky during a stormy night. He realized that he simply cannot put these emotions into words. The feeling of despair enclosed around his throat.

"Ok," choked out Raza. "You both have clearly thought this all the way through. So, I will trust my parents."

"Very good, my dear," commented Jiya.

"Perfect, my son," said Kunal.

"I must use the restroom," said Raza, "please excuse me."

Raza tried to collect the UCLA material.

"Let me dispose of that," said Jiya.

"And son," said Kunal, "your mother and I are very proud of how you played today. Steadfast and with purpose."
"Thank you, father," responded Raza.

Raza then removed himself from the exquisite mesh table. He pushed the chair back in place and walked towards the house. On his way inside, Raza felt rain drops on his shoulders. However, he is so concentrated on his thoughts that he doesn't notice. Once inside his house, Raza headed back upstairs to his room. There contemplated what had just occurred.

NOW
WHAT

*And when the two youths met the heart
of Hamilton beat like a drum. - A*

Lorenzo and Arianna are in the family restaurant kitchen.
Under the bright ceiling lights Arianna is prepping for tonight
and making Lorenzo a meal. Lorenzo, on the other hand, is in
a dejected mood while trying to finish his academic English
homework.

Lorenzo is alarmed at the state of the kitchen. While doing
homework in his room he felt famished, so he grabbed his work
and headed downstairs to prepare a snack. He didn't expect to
find the kitchen and his mother in such a busy state.

When Lorenzo joined his mother, Arianna informed him that
the restaurant was doing an impromptu soup kitchen. Tonight, in
several hours, *for* several hours. In response, Lorenzo sat down at
the table, well away from his mother's work and began finishing
his homework.

"So, mom which character is Hamlet's foil? And," Lorenzo read
aloud, "how does symbolism and the foil apply to this scene?"

"Lo," Arianna curtly said. "I'm trying to prepare for the soup
kitchen tonight. I can't help you with that, but I can help you with
this."

Arianna presented Lorenzo with her traditional homemade
hamburger and fries. It came dressed according to his taste;
lettuce, tomatoes, onions, ketchup and pickles. The still steaming
home cut fries were nice and crispy.

Lorenzo was encouraged from the sight of the food. Arianna
placed a fresh glass of water down beside the dish. The ice clinked
politely as the water settled down. He pushed his homework away
and promptly attacked the burger without mercy.
"Fanks," said Lorenzo in-between assertive bites.

With her son now eating, Arianna returned to her preparations. Behind her atop the efficient oven, were three large pots. Inside boiling was the base of the soup. With the turn of a dial Arianna lowered the temperature of the stove so the soup could simmer. Then, she began peeling potatoes.

Lorenzo asked, "Why are we doing an impromptu soup kitchen?" And right before Arianna could respond he quickly added, "If you and dad are getting divorced?" He then carefully took a sip of water.

"Great question," began his mom.

Arianna's back was facing her son and her attention was presently on the stove. The smell of the soup was becoming tantalizingly pungent.
Arianna was making a Bulalo soup (bone broth), a chicken stock soup, and some Minestrone. In response to her son, she put the peeled potato down on the counter with the rest. She thought about his pertinent question. It tired her immensely. She too was unsure of the choices that lead up to this event. Lorenzo's question also reminded her of the life spent with Carmine. All in all, it was not terrible. However, it ended up being wrong.

Lorenzo swallowed the rest of his food and when he looked at his mother, he saw Arianna's composed face.

"They are invasive questions as well," said Arianna.

Lorenzo gulped the rest of the glass of water. The ice cubes had yet not melted.

"Furthermore, why are you so suddenly interested in your father's and my affairs?" She paused for a brief second. "When we announced the decision to get divorced, you were loud. Since then, you've avoided us like a plague." Her voice was fair and reasonable, and her hands were balled into fists which rested on her hips.

Satisfied with her questions, Ariana waited for her son to respond.

Lorenzo blinked several times in quick succession and then said, "So you're just going to deflect my question? You said they were great."

Arianna was impressed at Lorenzo's confidence.

After a deep breath Arianna responded, "Fine. We are doing this, this soup kitchen, despite the divorce, because I want to give back…to the community, before I leave the restaurant. Your father has been happy to indulge me in this. When your brother gets back, I plan on asking him for assistance. Although he might be too tired from his soccer game. Would you be interested in helping?"

While talking to his mother Lorenzo felt an acute discomfort in his chest. Lorenzo knew himself that he had avoided his parents. The divorce and the changes it would bring scared him immensely. He did not even think of that possible future. Could not fathom it. A future of two houses, two Christmases and two families. A future of if his parents and new partners. The discomfort slowly became a piercing pain.

Additionally, Arianna's request ruined Lorenzo's plan. He had already made plans with Tipsy Pixie. In the late afternoon they were to meet up. In fact, she was going to message him the location soon. Then Tipsy Pixie would provide a special service and Lorenzo would gain the respect of the Snake Detection Hypothesis.

Lorenzo cleared his throat and said, "I'd love to help but I can't. I have plans tonight."

Unconsciously, Arianna's left eyebrow raised, and her arms cross her chest. "Do these plans have anything to do with $500?"

Lorenzo choked and coughed. He recovers quickly and said, "Wouldn't someone leaving the restaurant need $500 the most?"

"What are you insinuating?" asked Arianna, coldly.
"I'm suggesting that you should look harder," said Lorenzo flippantly. He then removed himself from the kitchen table and stood on his feet.

"Where are you off to?"

"Don't worry about it."

The dryness in her son's voice startled Arianna into silence. Arianna thought, *how did he know the $500 was missing?*

With his books in hand, Lorenzo exited the kitchen and makes his way back upstairs. He walked quickly to his room and disregarded everything else. At the open door he threw his books at the wall and grabbed the wallet on the desk. The corner of the book's hardcover left a mark on the wall before it tumbled to the floor. Loose papers are strewn about. Lorenzo took no notice. He made his way out of the restaurant.

...

Later that day, at 6:10 p.m., Lorenzo is seated at the back of a city bus. He notices that outside the sky is grey. *It looks like it might rain*, he thinks. Blankets of somber clouds fill the sky. Inside the bus there are several people with baggage. One gentleman has a case of beer on the seat beside him and a lady has a cart of groceries. Dutifully, the bus driver follows his route.

Lorenzo reminisces. As he stepped out of the family restaurant, he received a message. Tipsy Pixie wrote that they could rendezvous at the bubble tea restaurant by the Hawk and Sparrow. Lorenzo confirmed that he knew where it was and that he would meet her there in ten to fifteen minutes. Tipsy Pixie replied with emojis and wrote that she would be wearing a pink hat.

Lorenzo waves to thank the driver and steps off the bus. He walks towards the rendezvous point. Lorenzo is three minutes away from the bubble tea spot. He thought he would be more nervous. Like butterflies in the stomach nervous. But all he feels is guilt in his gut that rests there like a hard stone. To distract himself, he takes in his surroundings; while the sky is grey, it is still bright out. The downtown street is exactly as he remembers. The verdant sidewalk trees and greenery appear healthy. Common brown birds are chirping pleasantly to one another. The storefronts are clean and tidy, and the streetlights are already illuminated.

Lorenzo sees the bubble tea establishment; it's across the street, and through the main window, he can see that it does not appear busy. He glances both ways and takes a deep breath before crossing the street.

He opens the bubble tea door and as it opens, a small bell chimes pleasantly. Behind the counter, a single worker notices Lorenzo's entrance; the energetic girl waves politely. Lorenzo waves back and observes that she is wearing a purple hat and matching purple apron. She continues to stack plastic cups into their spot.

Lorenzo walks deeper into the restaurant. The lighting is dim and nonthreatening. His nose picks up the soft smell of green tea and he notices that, inside, it is quite chilly. His ears hear some catchy pop music, *is this BTS?* Thinks Lorenzo. He sees the clear and vibrant menu above the working girl. The print is large enough to be read from the entrance. Behind the employee Lorenzo can see various juice machines and fresh ingredients. There is a back door where he assumes leads to the kitchen. The rest of the space is used for seating. He likes that the whole place follows a purple and white colour scheme.

Deeper Lorenzo goes. At the back left, in a secluded booth, Lorenzo sees an attractive girl wearing a pink hat. He makes eye contact with her and waves.

Sophia Reeves (Tipsy Pixi) see's Lorenzo Cavallone (Lil' Lion) and waves back. This is their first meeting. However, little did they know, they have passed each other in the high school hallway several times. Additionally, during those brief moments, Sophia's perfume made Lorenzo sneeze twice.

She notices that Lorenzo is wearing a short sleeve navy-blue shirt with a wicked shark on it and black jeans. He enters the comfortable booth and sits down right across from her.

Lorenzo notices that on the table there is a half-finished green tea drink. It sits in front of Tipsy Pixie. She is wearing a pink tube top with a loose white cardigan over it, around her throat is a white choker, and, on her head, backwards, is a pink baseball cap.

"Lil' Lion, shall we get right to it?" asks Sophia. Her voice comes out sweet as caramel.

Lorenzo's eyes open wider. "R-r-right here?" he asks.

Sophia laughs at his innocent response. Her laugh is authentic and light. She responds, "No silly. I mean let's discuss why we're here."

"Oh, of course," replies Lorenzo. "S-should I call you Tipsy Pixie?"

Sophia smiles and sips her drink.

"Hmmm," Sophia begins. It almost sounds as if she is purring. "I feel it's better if we call each other by our usernames. Pixie is good, and I like Lion for you. You know anonymity and all that."

Her thoughts were on the fate of Kassandra. Her expulsion was a serious consequence.

Meanwhile, Lorenzo is infatuated. He is utterly spellbound by Pixie. If she asked him to bark like a dog, he would. If she asked him to crawl on all fours, he would. If she asked him to have sex with her, he definitely would.

"Lion? Did you hear what I just asked?"

"Umm, no," answers Lorenzo, "I was distracted by how b-beautiful you are." He says meekly.

"Aww thanks, honey; I asked if the price is still good."

"Oh ye. I have it all here." Lorenzo pats his jean pocket where his wallet is. It rests uncomfortably in his pocket. He, and his wallet, are not used to carrying around that much cash.

"Where are we, uh, where are we going to," Lorenzo looks around the place and whispers, "do it?"

Sophia is unperturbed by Lorenzo's question.

"Don't you worry." She winks at Lorenzo. "Pixie's got it all figured out."

...

Twenty minutes later Lorenzo is inside the Reeves apartment

living room; It smells welcoming, like freshly baked goods. He is seated on a comfortable sofa with a ceiling fan directly above him; it is moving at a peaceful pace. Natural light is spilling in from the East window. To Lorenzo, the whole apartment has a tranquil atmosphere.

Sophia truly had it all planned out. The walk from the bubble tea spot took ten minutes. She made sure to walk in front of her client and lead him up the stairs. Marge Reeves was working an overtime shift, so she would not be back at the apartment until tomorrow. In her room, Sophia was currently changing into the lingerie she had recently purchased. The feeling of a plan coming together pleased her greatly.

On the back of the closet door, she checked herself out in the full body mirror. Sophia's long hair was shining, and she thought the light blue velvet bra and panties made her look sexy and mature. She pushed her breasts up and felt the sensual material on her skin. Her hands felt hot. She smiled and took one more look at herself before donning the robe and tying the belt around her waist.

Then she made sure her room was in order. Sophia saw that everything was in place; her desk was spotless, her bed was made, all the loose clothes were put away hidden, out of sight, behind the other door of the closet.

Before she called in her client, Sophia tiptoed to her desk. She opened a drawer, removed a dark green candle and a lighter. She ignited the lighter and brought the flame to the wick. Sophia placed the candle in the center of her desk and in moments the room would smell of evergreen trees. One of her most favoured aromas.

Like a gazelle she jumps on to her bed and now, with everything in order, Pixie says, "I'm reeeaaddyy. You can come in nnooww." Lorenzo's heart is thumping madly. He swears he can feel the blood circulate his body. It takes all of his mind power to get up from the couch. He imagines that Page and Ray have sex all the time. *So, it can't be that difficult,* Lorenzo thought. He walks towards the door. *Plus, it's supposed to be fun. The fact that I'm paying for it doesn't change that.* He earnestly hoped. Lorenzo reaches to the doorknob. *Here goes everything.*

KARAOKE
MANDATE

*Do not deny your heritage. We all pay for
the violence of our ancestors. - A*

At exactly one in the morning, Lorenzo Cavallone finds himself
taking a shot of rum. Under the familiar disco ball lights, the
Zhang's garage is in a jovial mood. It also contains a lingering
smell of marijuana. The company present are just beginning to
start their revelry. As the spirit touches Lorenzo's tongue, he is
unable to mask his face. Thus, he produces an honest grimace.

"He he ha! He he ha! Woah! Your face! Lo'!" Page says. Her
unusual laugh and her teasing tone gets the attention of everyone
present.

Dylan and Deckard Zhang turn their attention to their young
friend; the look on Lorenzo's face produces full smiles on theirs.
They do so in unison. It's during these moments when the band,
as well as Lorenzo, find difficulty in telling the brothers apart.
It doesn't help that the D's are both wearing matching outfits,
dickies long sleeve coveralls in navy blue.

At the request of their parents, the brothers have basically spent
the whole day on a single task. In-between smoking and eating
breaks the twins finally finished repainting the workout room. It
was now a solid coat of gold. Some residual paint could be seen
on the sleeves of the coveralls.

"My dude, we only have this huge bottle of Kraken," Dylan says
while smiling. His wicked mohawk has been dyed white. A tiny
bit of gold paint is in his hair, and it reflects off the disco lights.

"Hopefully the taste grows on you," Deckard comments while
smiling.

Ray is the last to turn his attention to Lorenzo. He says, "I missed
it! Let's take another shot. We forgot to toast anyways."

Now recovered, Lorenzo says, "How unacceptable! To have forgotten to toast. We bring the wrath of Bacchus upon us."

Not catching any of the sarcasm Ray responds, "See gang? Lo' wants another shot." In the air, with his right index finger extended he makes a pointing gesture. "Another one!"

Page rests her hand on her boyfriends' shoulder. "Settle down D.J Khaled," she says. However, she nods her head at Dylan, and he begins to repour the Kraken. Not for the last time the dark liquid fills the glasses.

Similar to the rum, Ray and Page are dressed in equally murky colours. Their faded black short sleeve shirts are matching, and they are both wearing tight black jeans. Rays are ripped at the knees. On their feet they both wear black vans. Additionally, Ray is wearing a shiny chain necklace with a crucifix on it and Page has a black ribbon tying her hair back.

Meanwhile, Deckard is preoccupied. After the first shot of rum, and after reviewing Lo's funny face, the drummer returned to the tall fridge. Beside the tall fridge there is a sensible wooden table, a flat screen T.V. and The Zhang Karaoke Machine.

The infamous Zhang karaoke device has been passed down for exactly four generations; it is one of the very first Chinese models. The compact rectangle looks like a retro gaming system. There are minor dents and shallow scratch marks on its case. Like battle scars, the wear and tear on the machine is proudly worn. And although ancient, the ingenuity of the Zhang family has kept the song list of songs up to date. With a keyboard attachment, Deckard is finishing the final touches.

"Remind me, what are we celebrating again?" asks Dylan. He had just finished pouring the final glass with rum.

"We are celebrating," began Page. Her tone was of a tired reminder. "Landing a motherfuckin' agent."

"Lit," Dylan responded.

Observing, Lorenzo was fairly sure Dylan already knew the

reason they were celebrating. He simply asked because he wanted to hear it spoken aloud.

"Shots are ready," said Dylan.

"Karaoke is ready," called out his brother.

The lead guitarist clapped her hands three times and then said, "Toast!"

"Gather around," said Ray.

The Snake Detection Hypothesis and their high school friend surrounded the lead singer. Each had a shot of rum in hand.

"We have accomplished a great achievement. While we still have a long way to go; we have taken a step in the right direction. Okay, okay I'll hurry up. Babe, don't look at me like that."

"I *literally* just said what we were celebrating," said Page.

"To getting an agent!" cheered Ray.

"Here!" said Dylan.

"Here!" said Deckard, a heartbeat later.

"Agent!" cheered Lorenzo.

Altogether, they took a shot of Kraken. Most of them savoured it and some of them abhorred it.

"Holy!" pointed out Ray. "Har har har."

Lorenzo's face made the same grimace. With haste he presented the band his open mouth. Proof he finished the shot. During this time, Page was happy that her face went unnoticed. She also disliked the rum and was unsure if she was successful in masking the antipathy from her face. Meanwhile, the D's faces were as lit as Rudolph's nose.

"Karaoke!" The D's say in unison.

...

Songs later. Shots later. About an hour later, in the Snake
Detection Hypothesis's base of operations, Lorenzo is sitting on
the comfy leather couch. He is listening and watching the D's sing
a pirate shanty. He is fairly sure that this is their third song in a
row. Beside him, kissing on the couch, are Ray and Page. Under
the disco ball lights, Lorenzo silently judges that if passion could
be a number, out of ten, the couple's performance was a solid,
sweaty seven.

"The bounty hunter no one saw," sang Dylan. While singing into
the mic his voice was amplified by the speakers on the television.
His voice filled the space.

"Debts settled with Shock and Awe! Here begins the ballad of a
fiery fortuneee," sang Deckard into a matching mic.

Silently and appreciatively, Lorenzo judged that the D's enjoyed
karaoke.

Climbing the rank, they said it all sank!

Come one, come all.

Only had himself to thank, here lies Gangplank!

Come one, come all.

The sea shanty sends Lorenzo's thoughts inward. He feels a lot.
Physically, his face is hot. His stomach is irritated and nauseous.
It is as if he is presenting a book report in front of his class for
the first time. Yet, his head and limbs feel weightless. Mentally,
his thoughts swim uninhibited. He does not have the emotional
intelligence to put his feelings into words. And while he cannot
describe them, they are ashamed guilt, a deluded sense of pride,
and a faux happiness. *What is wrong?* Lorenzo thinks.

Gather around and keep yer pound,

Ay you sea dog! Settle down!

They're building his mound,

Miss Fortune put him 'n the ground.

Lorenzo buries his face in his hands. Drunkenly, he attempts to recall what he did yesterday. The thought sends blood down to his legs. *My hand opened the door and then, and then, I saw an angel. She called me over to her. It smelled of evergreen. And then we did stuff*, he thinks. To prevent a full-on erection, he chose to skip ahead. *And then I left the money on the desk. By the candle.*

Lorenzo notices that his hands are hot. He also notices that tightly wrapped around his right hand is Pixie's blue velvet belt. Stupefied, he brings it to his nose. He smells lavender and a hint of evergreen. *It even smells of her.* He feels crestfallen. *I took it from her, like I took the $500.*

A hand wraps around Lorenzo's shoulder. It greatly flusters his thoughts. A lightning bolt jolts through his spine, and he sits up straight.

"What's that?" asks Ray. His lips are close to Lorenzo's ear. He can feel the heat of Ray's breath and can smell rum. The couple had unlocked lips due to Page's need for the bathroom.

"I don't want to talk about it," responds Lorenzo.

He's dead, he's gone, and we sing it in this song!

Her parents she did avenge when she got her revenge.

She'll be counting her fortune,

Don't mess with Miss Fortune!

Climbing the rank,

They said it all sank.

Gruesome goner Gangplank!

The D's finished the song. They fist bump and move to the machine. The twins then hold a hushed discussion. It was about what song to choose next.
Ray removes his arm from around Lorenzo's shoulder and backs away to a reasonable distance.

"Don't kiss and tell, eh? Respectable, Lo."

"Something like that. Wait, how did you know?"

Lorenzo looks to Ray. He sees the lead singer in a relaxed position. He is stretched out. His hands are behind his head and his feet are atop the solid coffee table.

"That's from a girl. Right?" Ray asks. He takes Lorenzo's silence as confirmation. He closes his eyes and says, "You know, young grasshopper, this makes you a man now."

"A man?" Lorenzo asks.

"Yeah, that one!" says Dylan excitedly.

Another song begins to play. Page enters through the house door. She is distracted by the song and leaves it open.

"Fuck it!" she says, "we'll do it live!"

The tipsy bassist then walks over to the twins and snatches the offered mic.

"Ha ha why did you say that?" asks Deckard.

Ignoring the insipid question, Page doesn't miss a note.

Dogs are made of barks and sticks,

While cats are made of twilight and tricks.

And in the dark it's hard to think.

"Yeah dude," Ray continues. He moves closer to Lorenzo so that the karaoke does not impede the conversation. "You did the do. You're a man."

Lost without light,

Years spent on the same plight.

I long for your sight.

But in the dark it's hard to think.

From the lead singer's tone Lorenzo feels he's speaking about simple math. *One plus one equals two, duh Lo'.*

"Nice. Thanks. I feel like a man," Lorenzo lied. Truly he does not feel like a man. If anything, he is repulsed. Lorenzo blinks and the music is paused.

"Ayo?! The fuck you doing?" asks Page. Her tone of voice is thick with aggression. She even threatens to strike her boyfriend.

Ray effortlessly dodges away and takes the offered mic, he says, "Thank you, Dylan." His voice is needlessly amplified, "I asked him to pause your angelic singing to make a toast."

"I'm literally going to make out with you to shut you up," threatens Page.

"We can after," promises Ray smiling. "Trust me, it's for a good reason."

Page's body language suggests temporary patience. Silently and angrily, she awaits to hear the reason that interrupted her turn at karaoke. Following her lead, Deckard begins to pour another round of shots. The large bottle of rum is exactly half empty.

Meanwhile, Dylan halfway unzips his navy-blue coverall, folds the arms around the back of his waist, and ties it off. Underneath he is wearing a white tank top. It matches his white mohawk. Lorenzo, still seated on the comfy leather couch, stares directly at the disco ball. He is reminded of constellations.

Ray waits until everyone has a glass before he begins his toast.

Begrudgingly, Lorenzo stands up to join the band. The Snake Detection Hypothesis' drummer hands shots out to everyone. Page, the D's, and Lorenzo are in a semi-circle surrounding Ray. As soon as everyone is ready, he says, "We have accompli-"

"You literally said this already," cut in Deckard.

"Why are we doing another toast?!" demanded Page.

"Here! Here!" said Dylan.

With his head already swimming, Lorenzo is bemused.

"Wait!" says Ray. His voice is aggressively amplified. In a quieter tone he continues, "I remember now...I want to toast to becoming a man."

"I'm a man!" says Deckard proudly.

"Are you sure?" questions Dylan.

"Are you sure?" Deckard mimics. He does so in a condescending tone.

"No. Are you sure?" Dylan says again. He pokes his brother in the sternum. Some rum spills out of Deckard's glass.

"Heck yeah, I'm sure! Look what I can do." Deckard puts his shot glass down and then looks to Lorenzo. He holds his hand towards Lorenzo. Lorenzo is confused. He doesn't understand what the drummer wants.
"The ribbon," Dylan whispers.

Lorenzo looks to the blue belt; it is now loosely wrapped around his hand. He shrugs and hands it to Deckard. After a moment Deckard, while drunk, ties the belt in a complicated knot.

"The hangman's knot," says Page. "Wooow," her voice is thick with sarcasm. "Only a *real* man would know that one." She then throws back her head and laughs heartily at her own comment. Her weird laugh fills the space.

The D's make eye contact and Dylan says, "*Women.*" In agreement Deckard nods. He hands the belt back to Lorenzo. Lorenzo's eyebrows raise. He is genuinely impressed at the drunken feat.

With real vigor Ray toasts, "To being women and men!"

In unison, everyone downs their shot.

Lorenzo almost regurgitates. He feels disoriented. The disco ball lights are moving too fast. Internally, his repressed emotions are screaming.

"F-f-fresh airrr-r," Lorenzo says.

He says this to himself rather than towards any of the band members. None of the Snakes even register his voice. It's as if he is a shadow. In fact, Page and Ray are already making out and the D's are preparing another bong toke. So, while impaired, Lorenzo begins to stumble towards the open garage door.

On his journey for fresh air, Lorenzo almost trips three times. He steps on a red lighter but recovers. Then he trips on his own shoes. He maintains balance by the help of the garage wall; to Lorenzo the Zhang garage is spinning with disco lights. And the third time he falters is because the smell of fresh air disorients him.

Once outside, Lorenzo stands still and breathes deeply. The relief is immediate. After several breaths he drunkenly catalogues his surroundings. A car passes zips by on the street. It's dark outside and he can feel a slight drizzle. The Zhang driveway is clam and peaceful. He closes his eyes. Immediately, the dizziness and pain come back.

A low burp strikes. Alarmed and alerted Lorenzo opens his eyes and looks around in an effort to detect who burped. His ears hear another burp, but it sounds even deeper than humanly possible. Cautiously, Lorenzo moves towards where he heard the sound.

Right in front of the pathway to the Zhang backyard is a small green frog. The creature sits in a little puddle of rainwater. Music cuts through the soft sounds of rain. The band has started karaoke again. When Lorenzo makes eye contact with the frog, the frog belches again.

"It's just a little froggy," Lorenzo says.

"Ribbbbit!" says the tiny green frog.
In an attempt to burp back, Lorenzo almost vomits. He grasps is stomach and covers his mouth. After a second, he finds balance.

"Hellooo to you too Mr. Frog," Lorenzo croaks. "Ugh, I almost hurled."

In response, the little green frog turns around and hops down the shady backyard path. Lorenzo's eyes are glued to the creature. Its leaps are so graceful and precise. Without a second thought, Lorenzo follows the organism into the Zhang backyard. The sounds of music fades away.

The backyard is pitch black. The only discernable noise is the soft pitter patter of rain on the grass and cement. Lorenzo stands at the back-left corner of the Zhang house. His hand is resting on the side of the modern construction. He stands on the last bit of pavement. Before him is darkness and grass. Lorenzo squints his eyes; he can barely see anything. Abruptly, he hears the familiar frog sound. He guesses it must be deeper in the backyard. He hears it calling again. Emboldened by the Kraken, he pursues the call.

While walking deeper into the backyard Lorenzo's eyes adjust to the darkness. His legs also adjust to the uneven landscape. He is now at the farthest edge of the backyard. Before him is a line of trees and wild bushes. With his hands, Lorenzo reaches out and touches the tree right in front of him. He feels dampness and hard bark.

Once again, the frog call is heard. Lorenzo's ears hear it amplified. It's as if the tiny green frog is croaking into a karaoke microphone. Utterly perplexed, Lorenzo moves past the trees and wild bushes. He enters the forest.

The forest has a warm and wet atmosphere. Rain is coming down harder now, but the tall trees shield the boy from the worst of it. Bugs that zip by but go unnoticed. Along with the frog noises, he can hear an owl hooting. And after an unknown amount of time Lorenzo steps into water.

"What the fuck?" He questions. His voice is full of shock.

Lorenzo steps back and notices that he has stepped into a brook of cold water. His left leg, up to his knee, is absolutely soaked. He also notices that on the perimeter of the brook there are small, medium, and large frogs. All are different shades of green and a few are nonchalantly croaking. Lorenzo chooses to sit down. His back rests on a thick tree.

After a moment of contemplation Lorenzo Cavallone says,

With my mind lost in a fog,

I heard the call of the frog.

What a rouge and peasant slave I am?

Who toils while alone but a peasant?

Who steals but a rouge?

Here I rave.

Here before me is the river of Asphodel!

Its heat attracts the croaking souls,

Oh, woe is we.

Its fire has taken my leg!

Oh, how I would truly sacrifice my leg,

To simply remove these feelings of woe.

What did I sow?

Time moves in slow-mo,

These feelings do not lessen they grow.

And yet, I am a man!

What a piece of work is a man?

I have yet to understand.

If time leads to rust,

Then we are only made of dust.

Slowly, Lorenzo stands up. He climbs up the tree. A poorly placed hand grabs on a sharp piece of bark and Lorenzo cuts his palm. The pain is dull compared to everything else he feels. The blood is ignored; raindrops continue to fall.

The boy comes to a thick branch that is able to hold his weight. Avoiding branches and leaves, he creeps to its end. With the blue velvet belt, he ties the hangman's knot around his throat. It takes a moment for it fit right. He then ties the other end around the branch.

"Here goes nothing."

S.M.S.

Subtlety and self-control are the deadliest threats to us all. - A

Raza Singh stepped out of the shower. He is refreshed and clean. With a towel, he wiped himself dry. He put on an old white marathon T- Shirt. It belonged to his dad. In blue letters it read "Around the Bay" and on the back of the shirt, in a blue box, is names of several local sponsors. The Hawk and Sparrow is on there as well as the Cavallone family restaurant. Raza changed into the rest of his clothes and exits the bathroom.

He made way downstairs; Raza's hand trailed along the top of the glossy banister. Raza could tell his father is still tending to his garden. From the outside, soft Indian music floated gently on the breeze.

"Raza! My dear," called out Jiya Singh. "I require a moment of your time. In the kitchen here. Darling?"

Raza made his way to the kitchen. As he entered, he noticed the gigantic window behind the deep sink was open. It bathed the kitchen in warm light and exposed the full hot summer sun. He could also identify his mom preparing a cold beverage on the kitchen counter.

"You've showered," Jiya stated. "Thank the heavens."

Raza responded by rolling his eyes and made his way to the fridge. On his way he asked, "Did you call me in here just to treat me like your cooking?"

"Go on," Jijya implored. Atop the marble counter, she mixed ice into a milky beige drink. It clinks agreeably.

"To simply burn me."

In response, Jiya grabbed an ice cube from the drink and threw it at her son. Raza's surprise was genuine, and his reaction was razor sharp. He opened the fridge door; like a shield, it blocked the incoming ice projectile. The frozen cube thudded against it and landed on the spotless kitchen floor.

When Raza closed the fridge, Jiya was on the other side. After a moment of shock, he saw that in her hands, was the cold beverage and a letter.

"I was trying to cool you off," Jiya said. "You know, from my burn. Take it! It's for you."

Ignoring what had just occurred Raza asked, "Who's it from?"

"I heard that if you open it, you might be able to discover that," his mom said timidly.

Raza watched as his mom exited the kitchen. She made her way back to the garden where she'd give the cold drink to her husband.

Raza ignored his thirst and retrieved a knife from the kitchen drawer. With the knife, he slowly cut open the side of the letter. Raza placed the knife on the counter and slid the contents out.

Silently and alone, Raza read the letter. After several re-reads he was confident he understood the message; Raza was accepted to all three programs. In the upcoming fall semester, he could study one of three McMaster curriculums.

Raza was not surprised. He truly didn't care about his future academics. He was still hung up on the fact that his parents have mapped out his life without his voice.

In his pants, Raza felt a double vibration. The cellphone, in his pocket, interrupted his thoughts. Raza grabbed the device. Lit on the front of the screen was a notification. A text message from Liam Cavallone. He saw that the message was three letters.

"S.O.S."

MIRACLE
MONTHS

Individuals need difficult times and
oppression to develop psychic muscles. - A

The fall sun shines magnificently. After a long and severe rainstorm, the fiery ball finally appears in the sky. The orange, yellow and brown leaves are eager to receive the last bit of sunlight before completely withering away. Despite the dying season and the previous rainstorm, the sun's warmth makes it a nice day.

Rays beam through the east side of the fifth-floor hospital window. Lorenzo Cavallone's closed eyelids are annoyed at the bright light. He had been in this hospital bed for three arduous months. The lacerations around his neck and the significant bump on his head were treated immediately and the team of doctors agreed that Lorenzo had fallen into a self-injury induced coma.

In fact, the doctors involved the police and after some light investigation, Lorenzo's suicide attempt was unraveled, chiefly, by Dylan Zhang, Lorenzo's rescuer.

Lorenzo's eyelids twitch. Then open. His fatigued eyes see the sun. He is forced to squint. Everything appears hazy and ethereal. Looking away, against the wall, he sees his mom sleeping in a standard hospital chair. Under a comfy blanket, Arianna Cavallone is breathing softly.

A constant beeping noise attracts Lorenzo's attention. Slowly, he swivels his head and sees that the noise is coming from surrounding hospital machines. Following the tubes, he slowly confirms that he is attached to these devices. He also notices that there is a thick scar on his right hand. And as his eyes adjust to the daylight, Lorenzo observes that there are flowers and cards on the foot of this bed.

"Glad you're back," says a voice.

Carefully, Lorenzo turns his head to the direction of the speaker.

At the threshold of the door, stands Carmine Cavallone. Lorenzo's father stands tall. He has removed his glasses and there are dark bags under his eyes. Carmine's feeling of gratitude is immeasurable. His eyes are glistening.

"Thank God!" says a voice.

Lorenzo turns his head back to his mom. Arianna is now awake with thankful tears streaming down her equally exhausted face.

...

One month later, at the Cavallone family restaurant, it's raining heavily. However, inside, protected from the rain, are a plethora of cheerful individuals. These people are eating, drinking, and celebrating Lorenzo's miraculous recovery. Additionally, on a small make-shift stage, live music is being played. On stage is the Snake Detection Hypothesis. They are currently covering Journey's "Don't Stop Believing".

The fall rain began moments ago. The festivities began an hour ago. The planning began a week ago. And, thankfully, Lorenzo's health stabilized two weeks ago.

Two weeks ago, Lorenzo was allowed to leave the hospital. However, upon waking up, the boy's physical health was the subject of serious debate. He remained pale, unresponsive, and fatigued. The team of doctors were extremely sensitive. This was a delicate time. Between proper medication and the attention of his family, Lorenzo was guided through the shock of consciousness. Once his physical health became assured, his mental health was the next priority. Indeed, the team of doctors suggested he go to a weekly group discussion when he was ready. There he would be in a safe environment where he could talk about the feelings that lead him to attempt to take his own life.

A week ago, a welcome back party was forced. After Arianna's impromptu soup kitchen, the local community was strengthened. Unbelievably, within the neighbourhood, revenge schemes were forgotten, and a sense of unity was established. Furthermore, after the community got wind of Lorenzo's condition locals instantly banded together. Social media posts were posted, baked goods were baked and, while in the hospital, Lorenzo received numerous visitors. Additionally, these good friends helped prepare the family restaurant for this event.

An hour ago, Carmine stepped on the stage and said, "Thank you all for coming. Let me be brief. The unconditional support from the community has been a solid foundation. During the past unbearable months this foundation has kept me, and my family, standing. And so, to thank this community, words are not enough. *Please* enjoy the food and drinks. It's on the house tonight. Oh, and cheers," Carmine raised his drink. "To Lorenzo's recovery!"

...

The Snake Detection Hypothesis finished their song and exited the makeshift stage. In the meantime, from a laptop Liam set up, Italian music is played. The atmosphere of the restaurant is jovial. The band has earned a break to eat and drink.

Ray leads the band to a table close to the bar and the stage. There sits Lorenzo, Liam and Raza. In front of each of them is a finished plate of spaghetti and meatballs.

"Great set list," said Lorenzo. He took a small sip of wine.

"Truly," commented Raza. "Great cover choices."

"Let me clear the table," said Liam. "Come on Raza, help me man the bar."

"A drink would be nice,"

Once Liam and Raza leave Page said, "Stand the fuck up."

Lorenzo softly smiled and removed himself from his seat. He can see genuine smiles and glistening eyes. The band and Lorenzo embrace in their second group hug of the night. They hold this embrace for a solid minute. After the Snakes played music for half an hour, Lorenzo can feel their warm, sweaty heat–awkward. They disengaged from the group hug and sit back down at the table.

After a moment Ray said, "I wasn't sure you'd make it."

"S-shut up!" responded Page. She is shocked at her boyfriend's unfiltered remark.

"*What?*" continued Ray. "Lorenzo, for real, you were so pale."

"When I found you the next morning," said Dylan, "I thought you were already dead."

"We are dishonoured," commented Deckard solemnly.

In response Lorenzo smiled and said, "Well even if you are dishonoured, I'm grateful you saved my ass."

At the quaint bar, by the faux 2006 Italian FIFA world cup champions trophy Liam said, "Yo Raza, *thanks*, for having my back these last few months." While he has said this already Raza noticed that this time Liam's voice is full of pathos.

In response, Raza rolled his eyes. T*hat must be the wine talking already,* he thought.

"Bro, lets drink a glass of water and talk about something else," Raza said.

Liam poured two tall glasses of water. The two friends clink glasses.

"To the future," said Liam.

"To the future," said Raza.

They take a gulp of cool water.

"So, speaking of the future, what's our ace planning?" asks Liam.

Raza scratched the back of his head and said, "Well as you know I'm going to McMaster. So, you're looking at the future ace of the McMaster soccer team, *hopefully,* I guess. And I've sorta decided on becoming a marine biologist. You know fish and whales and sea lions and seagulls and..."

"Don't forget penguins!" added Liam.

"Yeah, haha, penguins too. What about you? What's in store for captain Cavallone?"

"Heh, I think I'm where I need to be. I'm going to help the family restaurant. Pay back the community. Plus, when Lorenzo's coma began my dad got a cat; I'm not exactly sure why he did, but the little bugger is a handful. She's already nipped my toes and fingers and shredded my socks and my dad's shoes."

"Can I see her? What's her name?"

"There's too much excitement for her right now. Plus, she's still a kitten. I can show you her tomorrow, if you're free. Her name is Iris."

"Ha. Great name."

. . .

Serendipitously, the fall rain stopped, and the celebration ended. While Carmine Cavallone does not officially kick anyone out, his final speech is understood. The jovial supporters get the message and, after their farewells, depart from the family restaurant.

After thirty minutes of priority cleaning, in the kitchen, around the new robust table, a serious family talk is being had; a solemn dialog that would change the Cavallone, and the Reeves family dynamic forever–awkward.

Sophia Reeves sits in-between her mother and Mr. Zhang. Dylan and Deckard's father, Denji Zhang, is a prominent Chinese lawyer. In fact, he is the sole reason Marge Reeves received reparations for the long-ago stolen money. Due to his effective wisdom, Marge deemed it necessary to ask him once again for sage counsel. A month ago, he was filled in on Sophia's plight. Denji benevolently accepted to give counsel and helped facilitate this meeting.

On the opposite side of the robust table, sit the Cavallone family. However, Liam is missing. After swiftly cleaning up, he left to check on Iris. Unsure on what the topic of conversation is about, Arianna, Carmine, and Lorenzo patiently wait for Sophia to open the dialog. *I lost her belt*, thinks Lorenzo, *I hope she's not here because of that.*

Sophia felt her anxiety building. In support, under the table, her mother held her hand. Immediately her anxiety was quelled. Marge knew what Sophia was about to say and prayed for the best.Unable to wait any longer Arianna said, "Thank you for coming." She then gave Lorenzo a deliberate look.

"Ah ye, I mean yes-um-yes I appreciate all your support," added Lorenzo.

"I've missed my last three periods," blurted out Sophia.

"That means, wait, what we did, no. Haha. I'm going to be a father?" asked Lorenzo in a defeated voice.

Carmine's hand is held his forehead.

"Who wants a drink?" offered Arianna. "No one, okay, sorry."

"May I ask why Mr. Zhang is here?" questioned Carmine.
"I am here to provide counsel," said Mr. Zhang. His voice is deep and sounds sage-like. "Too see with eyes unclouded. I am here to see the good in that which is evil, and the evil in that which is good. I attempt to preserve that balance."

"What do you suggest?" asked Lorenzo.

...

After the whole story is revealed, after some light banter, after some additional drinks, and after some mindful negotiating, a solution is reached. Although she had to swallow her pride, Sophia agreed to delete her FairySnap account. She also agreed to work at the Cavallone family restaurant, offering to fill in for Arianna when she departs. The Cavallone's are still getting divorced, but Arianna will only leave the restaurant after Sophia has learned the basics. Additionally, the child will be raised at the restaurant with the full support of everyone. And finally, Lorenzo and Sophia will begin a relationship.

FIN

Postscript

"Here goes nothing."

Lorenzo Cavallone, without thinking, throws himself off the branch. The blue velvet belt holds tight, and he is suspended in the air. Before rendered unconscious, he can feel rain drops on his face and the taut belt around his throat. His hands violently scratch at the belt before darkness consumes him.

Two long minutes later, a lightning bolt breaks through the dark clouds. The quick and powerful bolt of energy strikes the branch and severs it from the tree. Wood chips explode on contact. Thunder rumbles. While still unconscious Lorenzo falls into the brook of water. However, due to the velvet belt being connected to the branch, the boy's limp body follows the branch to a shallow levy of water.

Then, in the early morning, Dylan finds Lorenzo Leonidas Cavallone, utterly pale, barely breathing with a massive bump on his head and a cut on his palm. The rest has been already said.

FLASH

It has been a distinct honor to spend this time with you. I am humbled and grateful that you chose to spend your time with me. I wish you all the best and fervently pray that you find your own hammer to smash with and your own mountain to climb. Ciao.

WWW.PANDAMONIUMPUBLISHING.COM

Follow me on social media:
Instagram-@meeks_snakes
Twitter-@meeks_sneaks
Twitch-@meekssnakes